# Thimblestar

## A Faery Story

For my parents Beryl and Mick
and for Wendy my partner
and for Kyran my son

# Thimblestar

## A Faery Story

## M. J. Westley

**IMMANION PRESS**

Stafford England

**Thimblestar: A Faery Story**
By M.J. Westley
First edition © 2016

**ISBN 978-1-907737-72-5**

IP0124

Cover illustration: The Fairy Feller's Master-Stroke by Richard Dadd
Cover design and interior layout by Storm Constantine
Edited by Storm Constantine

Set in Palatino Linotype

An Immanion Press Edition
http://www.immanion-press.com
info@immanion-press.com

# A Most Important Introduction

Honestly, if I tell people my Grandfather was telepathically dictated an entire story by a faery no taller than a darning needle they think me mad. So I never mention it. Grandfather certainly made no mention of it—well, not verbally. You see, Grandfather returned from the 14/18 war only partially survived. He stumbled through the pandemic into a failed marriage, abandoning his wife and three daughters when the eldest was but eight. He popped out for cigarettes and was never seen by the family again. Well, not for thirty-eight years.

A chance meeting over a cuppa in a cafe in Worcester re-emerged him into the family consciousness—just. I met him twice during the summer of '66. In October that same year he was diagnosed with cancer—admitted to the Worcester Royal Infirmary where he died two weeks later.

He was an enigmatic reclusive figure. A raw-boned man. His skeletal stoop inclined toward the anonymity he preferred. His green eyes deep-set as though pushed into the clay of his flesh by the thumbs of a giant. His teeth false, his smile genuine. Carefree trousers, failing brogues, grubby waistcoat, collarless shirt. The clamour of the Great War, that had for so many years haunted his head, entombed beneath hearing aids so large they plugged the rims of his impressive ears like ceramic bottle tops. During our brief acquaintance he appeared to be surviving on a diet of beer, cigarettes and sterilised milk—a holy trinity that had reduced him physically to the meagreness of his pension. His home for almost forty years was a floundered, tiny wooden caravan, tilted into the corner of a large meadow, shaded by hawthorn and oak, adjacent to a pub at the edge of a tiny hamlet near Malvern. Time had capsized the caravan into a less than romantic situation, besieged by damp and rats. The week following Grandfather's cremation, it too was consigned to flames. Very little was saved. Two service medals, three photographs, a broken silver pocket watch, a waistcoat, a brass-buckled belt and a wooden box decoupaged with Japanese matchbox labels, which fortunately caught my eye by merit of their exotic designs. Tightly bound with garden string, this box had been secreted in a musty hold beneath his bed. The lid fastened tight by having a ribbon of wax poured along its seal. Strange embellishments indeed. Yet nothing compared to what lay concealed within. At first sight seemingly insignificant. A bundle of papers, rolled tight and tied with string identical to what fastened the box. Free of their bonds and unrolled, the papers revealed chapter after numbered chapter of beautifully scripted paragraphs. These were attached to an introduction written in an altogether different hand. Almost illegible in comparison. This was dated 'Summer 1942' and signed by my Grandfather. It opened with this salvo of a declaration:

*Whether you believe what I am about to tell or disbelieve, I care not. That it can be proved or disproved as a fact or fiction, I care even less. For it is my story and mine alone. Given to me by warrant of the pain which burdened my life. Not the lives of others. My life. I was the one they chose. The one they confided in. For thirteen years they whispered in the dark the telling. So was I sought in many ways. What they know of us is more than can ever be told. And what I know of them is more than you deserve.*

So begins Grandfather's introduction to the story of Thimblestar. A story containing confidentialities that to this day remain as obscure as his life. A story not written by my Grandfather, but given to him by an elemental—a faery—in his own words no taller than a darning needle, presumably via some form of telepathy. He described their first encounter thus:

*I sat up. I listened. I focussed on the farmhouse lights through the trees. I looked up at the waxing moon. I watched the assembling bats, unusually active at my end of the field. I retired to the caravan, closed the door and lit the oil lamp. The flame, perfect as a yellow bowl of sunlit glass, was as still as the night air. Suddenly it flickered and there she stood. No taller than a darning needle, I swear. Skin white as chalk. Hair red as blood. Eyes black as jet. Attired from neck to ankles in the harness of a mottled coat. The next instant she was vanished. Was I the victim of some trickery? So quick and quiet was the tiny spectre come and gone on the table.*

The following paragraph contains the crucial description of how he received the story—presumably preceded by a period of increased activity of which there is no record:

*She began to implant the sounds of words into my mind later that year. Able by her mere presence to induce a kind of gentle trance. A pale soporific state of mind. There was nothing adverse about this. In fact I welcomed it. Within half an hour of her vanishing into the night I would put pen to paper, transcribing in an almost hypnotic state the words she had so delicately cast upon my mind. Not until morning was I able to read what I had written. This is how the story in its entirety came into my possession. Each visit represented by a single chapter. Seventy-seven in all, spanning thirteen years.*

Charlie may have been a wilful man but he was not divisive. To what ends could such a complicated deception serve the seclusion of his chosen life? For all his education, he was a labourer. He worked, drank and slept between the ghosts of his faltered past. He had an overwhelming preference for seclusion. Where in all this desire for isolation and non-communication does the impulse to fabricate such a story exist? As a fact or fiction, personally I believe the case will always remain impossible to prove. Did Thimblestar and other elementals (he mentions 'them' and 'their') physically appear in his caravan or were they entirely imagined? Are things any less real when formed by an imagination so assertive that they can alter your life? Real or imagined—however we choose to define or separate the two—there is no denying Charlie's affections for Thimblestar. Much remains unanswered. But it was never the intention of this preface to conduct an exhaustive enquiry into every claim and corner of the story; that would require a hefty book in itself. Grandfather's sketchy introduction in its entirety consists of just the four paragraphs included here. Indicative of his life. So much left in the shadows. So much that is unaccountable. But appropriately so, I think. For the story will always remain a mystery. Inextricably linked by its strange imagery, symbolism, plot and language to the life of my Grandfather. It was his story—and his alone. And I can understand completely his desire to guard it, hide it and keep it secret. However, I also think that with his death the mysterious bonds that warranted such secrecy were severed and the story set free (so to speak) on its own terms. Grandfather must have given this some thought when he penned those brief but indispensable paragraphs explaining its provenance, the final one of which provides us with the most suitable end to this rather irresolute but necessary preface:

*That her visitations rescued my sanity and possibly saved my life I remain convinced. Yet I was never remorseful at their ending. My soul was the recipient of a happy intervention. To call it divine may seem extreme, but it was divinely suited to my needs. The meditative affections relayed by her attentions helped me re-equate the events of my life into a semblance of order. As I finally came to an understanding with my past, all the uncertainties of the future appeared less threatening. I have her to thank for that. As she vanished on that final evening I instinctively knew our paths had irreversibly parted.*

C Ward
Summer 1942

# The Story Of Thimblestar
## As Told in Her Own Words

*Sempre il mal non viene per nocere*

# 1

Born in starshine I was. Baptised in a silver Georgian thimble. So my name found itself: Thimblestar. Not shapeless or murderous but fair of tradition. Eyes dark as mulberries prized. Skin flight white. Lepers and lions point the way, the peacock, the tree, the wolf to slay. As an evil spirit must chose evil, I was clean born to promised order in the roots of an ancient oak. This my domain. Edged on great woods where lords work. Four wings, not two. Small to thee, but not to me. For I know of those who can fly through the eye of a needle unmolested. Kelpies to the west there be. Yarthkins to the east. Redcaps dreaded north there dwell, spriggans south. Yet this coat covet my possessions. No more can Annis dread this realm. For the unicorn and the king's son embroidered here have secured our pasts and futures. Beware, this smallness you see before thee so spritely perched contains great magic. Cautions all will need to heed when summoning a faery deed. I think that you will fear me not, for thou hast gone topsy-turvy in the time of men and unbeknown to thee the searchings of thy soul hath found me out, not vice-versa.

## 2

Once a story always a story. Gathering the sediment of the world to its bosom. So here beginneth mine and thine.

I awoke from cold's great slumber to a spectacle no faery can tolerate—mess. Mess wide as a house. Coat-swathed in the cleft of an oak root secured I lay winter long, whilst unbeknown badgers blustered tooth and claw. Order was ransacked. My effects strewn. They ate my food entirely. Furniture too, so discordant is their diet. Upon my soul disorder was inflicted. Badgers have notorious manners. Fortunately their appetites ignore a faery's blood or badgers there'd be none. Nevertheless, tithes are tolled for these trespasses and blacksnout shall rue this intrusion.

Hall-fame racked with roots now conceals my door that welcomed all. My silver ruinously rubbed in dirt. Oak and steel should compare their sexes, for this house has withstood a thousand years of days. For that which high and low before the cock shall crow of faery blood none can miss, thou shalt search in vain all thy days. Round to round, far and wide are not the realms a faery hides. Seen only by those who need to see. Rades and weddings fair have chimed these roots. All thy physick and science would fail to uncover my door, so cleverly concealed is our world from the world of men.

# 3

Before the Saxon farmed away our oak and ash, my family found security in the roots of this our family tree. Ransacked by badgers, my ancient home was in truth small hurt. Nevertheless, a great misfortune did arise from this bungling invasion. The loss of my tea. Nose snubbed, paw rubbed, it lay scattered about the floor. So long spilt from its silver casket twas rendered ineffectual. This is not the tea I find thee sipping most evenings. Great magic hides within each leaf. Faeries confined would be, if not for the art of elfin tea. A powerful alchemy conceals its recipe. Stowed up, locked away, buried deep, secretly prepared from mushrooms ground, blue black eggs dried, then stored the elfin way in earthen pots bound with flax. Tis this tea alone that enables us to transport ourselves invisible. Beyond the sight of all things we freely move. Without it, many dangers would call upon our lives with malicious intent.

Elves prize anything artfully crafted. Most things our skills doth conjure we trade for tea. For it is we alone that can drink it. All else twould poison with vile convulsions of foul biles black, vomiting, swift followed by death. Tis therefore a trade of mutual benefit. Yet now I have none. The badgers have unwittingly destroyed it. This turn of unwanted events presents me with a dilemma. I be on one side of the great wood, the elves the other. To acquire my supply unaided by concealment would involve a journey of dangers great, yet options there are none. I must undertake it, or starve.

# 4

Watched I now with great intent for omens. For an owl's cry containeth doubt as to the wisdom of a journey. The spilling of wine or salt. Augury must with a faery's sense be tempered, else tis unmanageable. South and east a templum did I cast, which met with favourable manifestations. By this science I interpret the call and flight of birds into predictions. Tis a magpie that finally convinces me the time for departure is at hand. Flying right of centre, fresh filled with bloody spoils. I sing it a song:

*"Not a raven, not a dove*
*But half and half thee fly,*
*Unbaptised bird*
*That missed the flood*
*Must pride the devil's eye.*

*August is the magpie's month*
*Northern people say,*
*Drawn in flocks*
*Toward the dark*
*To farm the devil's hay.*

*Across the sea are legends too,*
*Farmland people know,*
*Seven hairs are the devil's gift*
*For the magpie's head to grow.*

*Not a raven, not a dove*
*But half and half thee fly,*
*Unbaptised bird*

*That missed the flood*
*Must pride the devil's eye."*

For akin to birds we are. We dance. We sing. We build a house. We fly. We receive man's ambivalence.

## 5

Sharpened I now my blades with bone and awaited the moon. Slowly she looped the wood with motherly light. Then did mask the water. Shoes of caterpillar skin to ward off illness, stitched with thread of moth hair, I placed upon my feet. Gloves and hat of bat wing supple, stitched with hair of bee. A necklace of silver buttercups linked beneath a linen shirt to dispel ill thought. The inheritance of my coat embroidered deep with tissue of gold, secured at the waist by a useful length of twine. Atop of this a long bow of pikesbone fashioned, taut-strung with a badger's whisker. Seven black arrows of hawthorn, flighted with wing of greenfly, secured to their murderous shafts with amber sap, poison tipped, I concealed within my coat. Washed I then my hands and face in a cauldron cold, before setting out to climb the tree that majestic sat above my history. For in this tree a bird there be. His name be Cybris. Black as a witch's hat. He may for trade fly me far. He may attempt to eat me. Or have me eaten if young are hatched. Yet Cybris though a trickster be has a preference for trade.

# 6

With wings tight-folded I began my ascent. By dawn I reached the base of his clefted nest and tapped as is customary three times with my bow to summon his attention. Old chackbill peered into my gloom from the soiled rim of his basket. Birds always talk with their heads to one side, so tis polite to balance the nature of conversation by closing one eye. I told him my destination. He appeared consenting and would oblige my plans for the trade of an (as yet) unsought favour. Using the twine that fastened my coat I created a girdle. Bound it then did I to his rump. On the count of three we were launched. Widdishanks we spiralled our fate. East headed. The wood a sombre strand endless spread. Air dread as winter's breath. Doom laden was our skies course. My feet and wrists stirruped in twine fast. The horizon mist muffled beyond boundless woodwave. Soon was our flight accompanied with raucous wheels flocked. Stated we our fates on a blade of iced wind. Not warmed by flight's exertions, well concealed was I within my coat. Thankful for the rising sun that began soon to face us, displacing the mournful eye of night. Twas for a while a weak affair, stony-faced. Then with appetite awoken did she ravenously devour the cold. Wheeling we ever east toward the source of this comfort, below us the wood a thousand colours lit.

Twas then a terrible and mighty shadow crossed my heart. Turning twas too late. The hind talon of the hawk already piercing my coat and tearing a wing. Cybris managed to deflect the full ferocity of yellow eyes' murderous intent with a tumbling action that saved my life from one threat by unseating me into another. Spun I like a magic top on a stone floor toward the wood's woven roof. Next, swinging from a hook of beech by my longbow anchored. Suspended I watched as up above Cybris attempted to catch the hawk in vain. Wheeling noisily away, complaining endlessly about the wicked assault, which of course had been aimed at me, not him. Rightfully upset, he rigorously pursued the darting hawk as it effortlessly outran his chastisements. Soon both birds were vanished above the canopy as I was abandoned to contemplate the mix of it.

I now found myself suspended above an unknown quarter of the world. Cradled by my bow swayed I no more than doth a cone or a pear bloomed into windsway. If a hawk had a man's sight twould be blindness to him. Best to be hid in a tree than the belly of yellow eyes. I made a pleasant enough decoration. Doth not the faery crown the tree? Dilemmas can be sneezed away if the snuff be ground from the tail of a werewolf. I produced a pinch from a casket of redhorn I keep in my pocket. Tis white and hot as lightning. Too much can reward thy greed with hallucination. Not the fondest of raptures. Can a gooseberry sneeze? If so, twould look as I did swinging. My coat opened out, bell shaped. My legs rocking to and fro like clappers. Thus I chimed away the whiles, sneezing by counts. Tis but worldswork.

Inspecting my wings revealed a small tear in the lower left. If I were to count myself fortunate twould be the smallest of sums. The morning was fast turning into imps' work. Rotating, I noticed a nest. Twas an untidy-looking platform but well enough for me to repair in. I unhooked my bow. Stealthily on all fours I crawled toward it, constantly gazing skyward. Twas an ugly unkempt affair much like the hair of a woodwouse. This one I afforded no courtesy. Tap it I did not. Crept I instead up its haphazard thatch. Producing my dagger I peeped in. Tis a constant surprise (though not uncommon) when what is outwardly ugly reveals within unexpected delights. Doth not the head of a toad contain a jewel? Or the pearl hide within the leprosy of a case? Three eggs, blue-green like faery glass. Brown dashed as though from marble wrought. Still warm. Tis obvious they are not abandoned. So where and who was the parent? I placed my hands and face against the warm shells. Gradually was I cuddled to drowsiness amidst these pretty ovens.

Suddenly was the air chilled anew. Twice now my heart crossed by threat in one morning. Looking up, did I see that which previously sought my life wheeling ever close. The air filled with alarm. I dived beneath her eggs, heart and mind at a gallop. The sky kecked. I had chosen the hawk's nest as a sanctuary. Cursing magpies and misguided predictions, I crossed my wings and fast gouged a dagger's hole into the base of an egg, large enough for me to crawl through. I then made a small incision at its top end. Luck had not entirely abandoned my quest as yolk (and not the leg of a chick) ballooned out of the larger hole, seeping into the nest's floor. Hastily I squeezed inside, replacing the discharge with myself. The deception worked. Yellow eyes sat above my white cloister all that afternoon and evening, unaware she sheltered and warmed that which earlier she'd attempted to kill. I repaired my coat. Cleaned my dagger. Then with a draft of vervain and hemlock distilled in a cask of beetleblack I bathed my wing. Twill repair but not overnight. Fortune continued.

During dark there came a storm, its belly bulged with barking dogs. Under cover of this commotion did I burrow through the nest's shallow base of larch and beech undetected. I deposited a portion of the debris inside the egg. Tis courteous to repay a debt. Then, in the small hours, unbeknown to my momentary mother, I made my escape, as pale pleasure renewed the horizon.

Tumble down the serpent's back misfortune shall thee find. Chestnut hath a dragon's skin. With apprehension I descended along its furrows. This is a game of snakes and ladders best left. Tis a rutty road unkind to cloth and skin. I was now in a realm midway twixt sky and earth. Safe hid by sails of shadow. Came I now to a parting in the bark. Splinter gashed, channelled to a hollow. I eased along its broken edge. Twas then my snout snipped frail smoke. This tree containeth fire. This funnel, a chimney be. Gingerly I gazed within. Black as a dragon's eye the hole stared back. Twas then I noticed a stairwell, almost hid in smokegloom, spiralling uneasily downward into the serpent's belly. A meagre shuffle of blue smoke crept out. Imperceptible as possible, I crept in.

The curvy wall was powdered with warm soot. It grew increasingly dark, each step less seen than the last. For a second time in one morning I paused midway. Looking up I again saw the dragon's eye. This time white, green-flecked. Taking charge of my longbow I armed it with an arrow black. Tis a notion for consideration when the sea doth drown in silence. Unexpectedly the chimney abruptly twisted then lowered into a half lit chamber. Twas not a faery place. Everything ill-suited. What's more, the entire cell was insulated with severed ears of mice, rats and bats, stretched and pinned by thorns to the walls. An ingenious insulation, providing the occupant with ample hooks for storage as well as warmth. Twas then a hand grabbed my leg. A three fingered manacle, wart-woven. Without turning I knew twas in fact not a hand but the foot of an imp. A foul imp. Misfortune greater than sipping water from a wolf's paw-print this dragon doth contain. Twould not be worse for him had he swallowed a bucket of goblin's ulcers. I turned to inspect this wretchedness. Twas of the white-skinned variety. Hands like feet, feet like hands. Teeth like hailstones, eyes like pimples of blood. White leggings torn. Jerkin of toad skin ripped. Green cape gathered in at a pocked neck by leather cord. A tall black hat atop a tall white face. A waistcoat of bird's-wing stitched. Hanging from his belt, leather caskets, a silver funnel, a dagger of hedgehog spine. He introduced himself as Lord Grimjaw.

Imps are pompous in the extreme and assume much. He invites me to drink. Famed for fashioning utensils out of beetles, the goblets produced are polished ladybird. The chairs: abdomen with legs of horn. He pours from a flagon of woodwine. I stare at the room's confusion. A necklace of insect eggs. A hat of plume moth. A splendid maggot horn. An assemblage of crucified beetles, bugs, moths, ants. Even a bee. Jars of rotten blackcurrant. Pickled worm hearts. Butterfly tongues. Stems of ragwort. A chestnut barrel of woodpeckers' beaks. Sacks of ravens' legs. Pots containing ash of fly. A stick o'staff. A sickle of grasshopper leg. Lord Grimjaw's obvious prize is his stove, constructed from a man's tin box embossed with harebell. He informs me that the word above the oven door spells 'pins'. He invites me to partake of his unequalled hospitality. I accept, whilst trying with glances to locate the stairs that have mysteriously disappeared.

What does an imp treasure most? I shall tell thee. Black diamonds. For tis by this unction they are afforded sight. Tis why they abode in dark. They have little need of light. Their world is illuminated by enchantment. Tis polarised within an amulet of black diamond usually worn about the neck. Removing it induces blindness.

Lord Grimjaw's neck is well bound. He prepares me a soup of ivy and willow. His preference is for pickled insect galls. This would account for his dung beetle breath. Yet the chamber has a tinder fragrance.

Suddenly the darkness is overrun with strange encounters. A head full of dreams doth ensue. Memories of an earlier life. A white bull doth serenade the world. Eleven times doth it orbit a moon of opal sombre. It swallows a star then chokes like a child. We toast it with libations siphoned through the bronchial tube of a weasel. Lord Grimjaw imbibes from a bowl of lead.

I realise my soup was tainted. Once again I find myself midway. This time twixt fleeting trances. Lord Grimjaw now appears with the body of an ox. He tows a plough fashioned from a stag beetle's antler. The seconds are changeful, his devices merely transient. I keep a mindful eye on his whereabouts. Tis well known that in order for him to sleep he will have to remove his amulet. For tis an eye that never closes. Obviously he has drugged me to conceal this ritual. He appears again sniffing profusely through the warted stump of his nose. Scratching the peninsula of his clefted chin with the toe of his foot. He removes his hat from the racked bump of his head, revealing a rough projection of prickly hair topped by a pimpled bubble of baldness. He collapses into the jet cradle of his beetled bed, fishbone sprung with mattress of marigold. Tis good to see him fall for tis less hideous than his gait. Imps walk with their arms. Long, pendulous, hard as oak. Their legs are withered bent structures with poutish knees, which they tuck beneath their bony carcasses, similar to a bird in flight. Nothing so graceful here. Waddling to and fro on hand-like feet, scratching its warts with feet-like hands. A curious spectacle. Grimjaw grips the footboard with his dextral toes. Yawning, he raises his leggish arms and tippytoes the wall. Slowly he unwraps his fingerish toes from the bed, curling his stunted legs beneath his chin. He unties his cape. My doped head falls against the iridescent table, overturning a casket of wine. Grimjaw looks up, smiles, then resumes his repose. I manage momentarily to raise my head and glimpse, within fireglitter, the amulet of gold and diamond black as he unties it from his neck, securing it in a purse of leather latched to his belt. Twould be murderous removing this grip. Tis obvious imps have a partiality for restraint. Rendered insensible, cloaked with paralysis, eventually I fell into the blackest of sleeps.

I have a sister. Her name is Winkleprimbell. She offers her charm through eyes of amber. Doth wolves enchant with hair like burning pine. Can cause a frog to laugh. Could single-handed wheel a mill of salt. Her words fired with yellow copper could coax a bread to water. What could I tell thee that she could not undo? Where doth a charm end and a curse begin? She hath a potter's hands crowned of nails garnet and amethyst. She would tell thee not to cut off thy nose to make a cup. We meet but once a year, which serves our affections well enough. For am I not me alive and not thee dead. Grimjaw's curse may be of his own volition. My sister would tell thee that it was well tied with ancient skill. Twould barely cause her wings to shrug. How doth this world rotate but on one axis. Yet north and south be worlds apart. Bound by infinities. So tis with she and I. As a man doth hide in a tree, and a bell within a man, so this bedevilment doth settle on Grimjaw's spirit like a template. Twas fortunate for me perhaps that he was cursed so. By removing his amulet he unwittingly erased the entire day's transactions from his life. Nothing for him will last more than a day. Be it good or evil. My memory of his misfortune is a recollection of something that arguably never occurred. Tis a paradox. Where doth a charm end and a curse begin? Imps are skilful with their handy feet but dull-witted. They applaud a routine of simple confusion. Perhaps tis benevolence not malevolence that enchants him so. His entire history is but a day of his making. Such a purging could a saint make. Tis hard to imagine a single fear surviving so short a life. He sleeps. He awakens. He replaces his hexed charm. All that was the previous day has evaporated. Tas gone as though in a dream. He remembers nothing.

Tis but worldswork.

Bluebells and moonshine doth lovers lure but dangers too. Expelled from Grimjaw's life, I awoke in a grove of birch and bramble dried. By the stars' numeracy I attempted to discover my whereabouts. These were less revealed than night's other agencies. I gathered my belongings and crawled beneath a fallen skirt of bark. I considered myself fortunate to have been cast into the base of the wood by Grimjaw's dilemma intact. My wings had suffered no further infliction. Not entirely free of his soup's intoxication, I slumped into the shelter to escape the unwanted attentions of owls and nightjars.

As my head began to nod in agreement with dreams' desires my left leg received a sharp kick. The offending foot was wrapped in a shoe of pressed foxglove. The shoes were attached to rootish legs that vanished neath a plain cloak of sack. This was topped out by the nut of an oakfruit face. Eyes like millet grain. A tiny cap of curled woodshave. It apologised for the abrupt summons and introduced itself as Hatat. Woodsprites are a furtive breed. They are sexless with heavy wide dormant wings, similar to those of a caddis fly, which they secrete beneath their drab vestures. As merchants, they enjoy an underhand reputation. They always transport their wares on beautifully crafted sleds of birch, harnessed to toads. This one was no exception, festooned with carved rapids of guilloche brilliantly coloured. All this in sharp contrast to the toad, which was as well turned out as any of that breed. This particular conveyance was laden with pots and pans. Standing only half my height Hatat was able to remain upright within the tunnel of fallen bark. It explained that I was about to nod off across a busy trade route. All the tunnels are well used by sprites to conceal their commerce. Most fallen strips of bark are appropriated thus. I enquired as to my whereabouts. It indicated that a favourable outcome may result from me accompanying its retinue. Lost, and with no hopeful alternative, I decided to tag along several paces to the rear, clear from the influence of its hazel rod – with which is mesmerised the toad – and the unclean air exuded from that creature's clumsy labourings.

# 12

Twas still dark when our procession finally stopped inside a wooden gallery. The toad rested its warty head on a green stone. Hatat loosened its noose of plaited horse hair. Next to this was a hearth of clay stone, which it swept clear of ash. It placed the smuts carefully into one of the tin pots. From a sack it produced strips of firewood. From a small tin, a pinch of yellow powder with which it dusted the sticks. Unscrewing the lid from an iron pot illuminated the charcoaled chamber with fireglow. Of any science related to wood doth sprites have insight. How doth the night but by fire depart? The hearth ignited, scorching the charred crescent of the roof. Tis said that a sprite could coax rain to burn. Contain fire within sealed pots they can. Tis topaz to them. Charms appear to defy the natural order of things, when in fact they are in agreement. Every lock has a key. The smoke was naturally vented through a fissure onto the stars.

Hatat prepared two cups of hawthorn tea. On the subject of tea, it enquired as to the reason for my visibility. Hatat was cheery enough but doth not a smile bare its teeth? Filled with apprehensions from recent events, I remained awake nibbling honeycake. Besides, a snoring toad could a volcano awaken. Twas a long event before moon and fire had paled away.

Hatat informed me that for trade it would consult the ashes of our shared fire. Sprites are famed for this science. The currency for such advice (were I to accept) would be the twine that secured my coat. My preference was to be short of a belt rather than information that may place me back on my intended course. I agreed. Hatat took the hazel rod and waved it slowly to and fro above the hearth.

"Sizzly, frizzly, crackly burn, reveal to thee what thy fate earn." It repeated this three times.

The proceedings were rudely interrupted as the toad lurched forward to swallow a spider, jolting the sled, spilling pots and pans. Hatat tapped it gently on the nose. Twas immediately pacified.

Placing the rod into the ashes, Hatat began to score a spiral design, revealing the clay stone beneath. "Dots, stars, dashes, fruit; scissors, a hammer, a lace, a boot. Daisies, scales, a house, a fan; ladders, scythes, keys if you can." It repeated this chant thrice also. It then blew onto the lure, hoisting a cloud of ash into the chamber. "Tis done. We must now sit and await the dust to settle."

"Thou who hast outlived man doth dial a shadow in his heart. Mimics thy divinity with stone. One eye should suffice when all that is thou containest."

Hatat gestured for trade. I handed over the twine. Twas then pleached to his hazel rod. Again he unscrewed the lid from the iron pot that contained fire. He plunged in the rod, stirring a bristle of sparks. The twine incinerated, but the rod reappeared unscathed. The indications were that a full disclosure would require another consultation. Hatat insisted that the first revelation had made it evident the entire manifestation was yet unrealised. Would I tag along? Pouring me a beaker of rosemary wine it pointed out that the route ahead was a merry thought. A trade ring. Something that cannot be compromised. At worst I would end up where I began. The toad has a single-minded compass. Tempted ever forward by nothing more than its own odour. A redolent ring for sure. I agreed.

The morning was ill-humoured. The ground cantankerous. The trees glowering. Tis fair to say I have seen happier gibbets. The grass cold-snagged with wind. Hatat opened a wooden chest to reveal a stash of catkin mufflers. Twas a day well summoned by woodpeckers. That afternoon, neath a fallen rowan, we ate berries red and hot as a gadfly's sting. Hatat boiled willow tea as sullen weather gathered on the world.

Twas a black event when the toad took its final lurch. For once I was truly glad of the sprite's company. We were soon assembled in the cleft of a willow's roots with a lively fire juggling shadows.

## 14

Lord Mauritius had a daughter
Who loved the vibrant tang of slaughter,
Set free the prey each day at six,
Count to ten then sharpen sticks.

Lord Mauritius had his spies
Who reported with frequency of cries
Arising from the great playpen
Where his daughter kept her secret den.

"Would you like to sit on my golden throne,
For one whole day quite alone?
Then allow me into your secret den,
I have not been there since I was ten."

"Alright my father, if you wish,
But take along a crystal dish,
Some knives and forks and spoons as well
And from the hall the summons bell."

Lord Mauritius had his spies
Engage the scene with great disguise,
They hid amidst the trees all ten,
Their eyes a crown about the den.

Entering there, quite alone,
His daughter meanwhile at the throne,
Did all at once the stench of blood
Fall down upon him in a flood.

Mislaid servants hung in twos,
In tidy rows their socks and shoes,
Their heads were stored in stolen boxes,
Each one marked 'bits of floppsies'.

Blood red sawdust hid the corners
With invitations to the mourners
Neatly filed and in their place,
Tied in bags of pale blue lace.

A decent gesture thought the Lord,
At least she isn't getting bored.

Tis an ancient verse. A cradle song. Tas enough of a twist
in the tale to stir the warmed flu milk we sipped,
inducing a lethargy into every weary bone. Twas told me
by my uncle, Blackthornbandyboots.

Hatat smiled. "A name as long in saying as his song.
Tis a delight for me to share a fire with a faery. Thou art
as well made and pretty as a wren's nest. Toads are
faithful, but no better made at the front than at the rear.
Discerning head from tail after a session of black beer is a
conundrum. Hopefully tomorrow shall reveal more of thy
whereabouts in this world."

Above us the night was mauled in stormlunge. Trees
rain-thrashed. Truly did our willow weep. Twas a fearful
collision, buffeting gradually away over the horizon, its
clumsy footfall eventually fading with the dark.

The morning prescribed fresh commerce. In exchange for my precious gloves, Hatat again marked out a spiral in the ash. "Milk, honey, wine, gold, mercury, salt and sulphur, reveal to me when all is told what thou shalt tell no other." Again twas thrice chanted. Again Hatat bound the gift to its hazel rod, baptising it with fire. The incineration disclosed a prophetic echo. One day more should our paths remain identical. Twould be an odd turn of events three quarters across a bridge to turn back. I decided therefore to continue.

Whilst Hatat loaded the sled and harnessed the toad, a check on my wing revealed it almost knit. With all my belongings in order and the day better blessed, we set off down the damp tunnel of a fallen tree. The toad always emerged from these cloaked byways better fed, the dark less inhabited. They endear themselves to sprites by token of their natural camouflage. An oddity when one considers they have in tow a chariot of rainbows. The brilliant livery however is a deception, amazingly no easier to spot than that which is cold-blooded and dull-mudded. Spritework vanishes into antiquity as doth a toad on a leaf.

Twas almost midday when we reached a clearing in the wood edged with anemones. With the toad completely static, apart from the pulsing balloon of his throat, Hatat stepped into the clearing pointing its hazel rod with outstretched arm along the perimeter of the distant trees. With skilful divination it pinpointed our destination. Crouching either side of the sled we set off. With my partners better hid than a miser's gold I thought it astute to conceal myself neath the parasol of a dead leaf. Supporting both edges with my hands, I raised it over my head whilst simultaneously holding my bow in my right hand and an arrow with my left. Toads can sprint well enough if encouraged, provided the sled's entire contents are well secured. Our first objective was a clump of mossy wood skirted with primrose. Upon reaching it we celebrated with a sip of rosehip wine. Unease distorts an open space though twere elastic. Hatat again took a bearing. We departed from the scented bank toward our next shelter, a fallen elm. The pace was brisk but not panicked. The air bright as a faery's wing. Imitating the dodman's humble crouch we scoured the court for malice. Without warning, the toad abruptly stopped. Twas so unexpected we overtook it. Tis undoubtedly a creature of limited repertoire concerning facial expression, but there was no doubting its trepidation. A great dread infected the air. Did all our bloods (not just the toad's) then run cold. Throwing the leaf to one side I armed the bow. Hatat dived for cover beneath the sled. Then did a fearsome blow strike my head with such severity that I was somersaulted onto the ground. Thus spilt, were my wits momentarily stunned. The hawk had approached extremely low, casting so close a shadow as to trick even the sun. We were entirely ambushed. With a fearful shock it struck the toad. Frozen with horror the poor creature's skin was gathered in by murderous hooks. Life and death doth momentarily embrace. The toad flinched with appalling distresses in that fleeting consummation. Having ruptured the toad's back the hawk then attempted to hoist its butchered prize into the air, thus twisting the sled and spilling its booty, most of which landed on Hatat, causing some injury, but simultaneously snaring its deadly talons in the toad's harness. With obvious trepidation I approached the grisly scene. Truly was the slayer trapped by the slain. Thus fettered I released an arrow into its flank. A chilled cry filled the welkin. Frantically picking horsehair with its barbed beak, it finally disentangled itself, freeing its blooded claws into the air. Obviously compromised by the poison injected from the arrow it eventually made an erratic escape into the wood's dark enclosure.

Fortunately Hatat swiftly regained consciousness. It gathered its scattered effects, clearly mortified by the toad's fate. Taking my knife did I then unbind the creature completely from the burdens of its life. Hatat would not be persuaded into the security of cover until it had despatched the toad in accordance with its obligations. With hazel rod he gently tapped the corpse eleven times between its eyes. Hatat then held a silver cask beneath the left eye with its left hand whilst the right hand tapped the eye of the toad twice with the rod, effortlessly causing it to dislodge from its socket and slip into the cask. It repeated this procedure with the right eye. It then brushed the entire carcass with salt. Hatat then secreted two stones inside the toad's jarred mouth. One white, the other dusted with red ochre. Finally, with great deftness, it removed the liver before cremating the remains.

"Weirdly weirdly weirdly writted, a toad is to love, not to be pitied, weirdly weirdly weirdly wrought, a toad befriended greatly sought."

After reciting these words, we managed between us to pull the sled into a recess neath the fallen elm. A natural veranda led to a grubby lobby that opened into a room of hall-like proportions. A sprite workshop, the entirety of which was overlaid with shelving. Each dusty support stooped neath regiments of barrels, tubs, boxes, baskets, kettles, pans and sacks. Inviting me to be seated, Hatat quietly unloaded the sled. Unscrewing the lid from the black iron pot containing fire cast a brighter aspect over our proceedings. We lit two seedhead torches, then boiled water for an infusion of dandelion root coffee. That evening the air was chilled as ghost breath. Hatat left the chamber returning to the embers. The toad was entirely burnt. Even the framework reduced to ash. Hatat recovered the stones it had earlier placed in the toad's mouth. Both were grey as blinded eyes. It then threw one toward the lowering sun, the other toward the rising moon.

"None can truly own another,
tis best to be kind, make him a brother,
for such desires are evil indeed,
spawned from envy, hatred, greed.

"Seeking such spoils as another to own
will unbalance thy soul with blackness sown,
tis a greed that's unnatural, enticing instead
a terrible forfeit of malice and dread."

We returned to the chamber.

That night did we dine on coltsfoot and fruit of mandrake with blackberry syrup. Neath the poppies' gentle trance did our traumas faint away.

"Poor Mr Lickspittle doth now a morkin be. Sleep in the shade of thy fallen arrow. I kiss thee farewell my unfortunate wart. Doth not the corpsehound call, the darkness fall? Doth not freedom of will invite by its nature a kinder approach to burdens shared? Tis less easy to declare thy fate a traitor without blaming oneself."

With this declaration Hatat folded into a fitful sleep. Twas an odd call but well meant.

Next morning did bring a conclusion to my own trilogy. Hatat again scribed the ashes, this time with a single line from left to right across the hearth.

"We three things disorient are, spit on thy friend for luck to go far."

It then spat on the sleeve of my coat. For interchange it required my hat of batskin. Having shared the same fate as both twine and gloves did we conclude the revelation. It placed in my hand a purse of weasel bladder. Opening it disclosed twine identical in length to that which I previously traded. Knit to this in three eyelets were three jewels of quartz, tourmaline and amber. These tokens were further enchanted with remarkable detail. The amber was clear but the tourmaline and quartz appeared to contain wizened hop-o'-my-thumb clothing. An adornment confirmed once held to the light. A tiny pair of dainty gloves and a hat in detail indistinguishable to mine own, fastened within the stone as doth a nutshell a nut.

Hatat continued. "For me to see and thee to be, an arrow should thee follow, thy journey's end beginneth here, pursue which bringeth sorrow."

Twas obvious from the prophecy that my destination lay in the direction taken by the wounded hawk. Hatat concluded with a warning for me not to misplace the purse containing the jewelled twine. Finally, did we kiss for luck, fairing each other well.

## 18

My grandmother's name was Marymerrylegs on account
of her strolling soul. She had white turbulent hair,
moonwaxed. Sang as doth the nightingale upon a slender
crescent. Did walk even when distracted by sleep. Fed me
owl egg soup, combed my hair in a mirror of obsidian.
Told me never in this world to fly visible.

"Twould not be worse for thee to place thy soul on a
trap-door. Or break thy reflection. Scry doth I with a
crystal eye or shick o' shack thine own tree, twould tell
thee the same. Never fly visible. As all things equal one,
tis certain thou'd be gone."

Twas advice well-heeded. Never did I rue, from that
day to this, her earnest counsel to attend. No less likely to
be deterred from this wisdom as was my path by
pearlwart, I set off on foot toward the hawk's sanctuary
of beechgloom. Moments later did I sprint into its cradle.

My mother's name was Sorsoonflittertrix. Lastly born
with eyes no less sinister than henbane. Could loop, spin,
roll and dive twixt the seam that separates night from
day. Contained more cures than that which cures all.
Could fill a hollow space with love, yet enter thy nose
with ease to twist thy words. Danced in skirts of
bindweed flower. Lived in chambers dark red, with
prizes of silver. Inherited ivory. As a child she drank
copious amounts of ginger and hemlock, smoked woody
nightshade through a pipe of fish gristle. Could fate a
hare, or hide (as doth a snail in a shell) in the stoop of a
hunchback. Sleepless as a nightingale. Tis from her I
inherited my desire to live alone. She herself came from a
long line of hermit faeries. Lived in the roots of a tree

more often visited by lightning than any else. Neath garlands of ivy and mistletoe. In fact, twas frequented more by people. A quality I am sure not lost on my mother, as this was an added deterrent for faeries. An odd call of a place. It stood isolated, in an ancient narrow field overlooking a valley. Tis no less a frickle than a frackle, as both past and future doth recognise a tree. Famed even as a child for precognition.

"As earth doth from water make repair, or Easter lift a king, as that which is must end for that to be, the world shall find this tree."

Tis her I have to thank for my ability to live alone.

I now found myself at the brow of a wooded ridge. Expeditiously I moved from tree to tree toward a darkened precipice. Twas difficult from the top to discover how far the bluff descended. Twas mazed as a labyrinth. Dark and damp as a well's eye. I adopted a more cautious pace. Twas well blunted with crags and scars. A place where entanglements are a common measure. Great bows of root swaggered down its hooded face. Requiring both arms for support I unstrung my bow and slipped it into a long pocket inside my coat. I gathered momentum. Wing folded yet fleet. Suddenly was the air loaded with gloomy whispers.

"Such a dark space for one so fair. A hasty foot can spell despair."

I stopped. I listened. Faeries know well enough when eyes are at work. Something was watching from somewhere. I continued my descent. Again a sullen shuffle of whispers filled the air.

"Such a pretty skip neath coat so rare. A hasty foot can spell despair."

Again I halted. Here were the trees so abundant, daylight was reduced to an ember's flicker. No more than a rolling glimmer. Faeries are too full of dark to fear it. I sat upon the lip of a rock comforted with moss.

"Tis a long way down from top to bottom for such a tiny soul to bear," the whispers hissed. "We can changeling a child or twist milk to bitter. Switch colour to suit thy religion. Tempt thy soul with nothing more than thine own reflection. Snip thy tail at the last hurdle, turn thine own immortality to dusty ghosts laying claim to some small fear."

Again the wood fell silent. Stepping from the rock I followed a tiny spring of bronzed water into a pebbled gully. Twas then I noticed, almost hid by a decayed canopy, a squat door of black iron riven into the clay bank. As cheerless a portal as one could wish for. Striking it revealed a resonance dull as lead. Twas well fastened and could not be budged. There was no key, handle, lever, recess, anything. Never did a doorway wish more to be something else. Suddenly the whispers returned.

"This is a door that refuses all, though each of us has the key. This is a door that opens for all, yet stoppeth only thee."

My sister can unravel a conundrum faster than tis tied. In fact, all faeries excel in this science. Thus twas I doused the iron with chance of water. Immediately it began to creak, though never did a door make more lamentations at thus being used, grinding and whining most reluctantly, revealing at the end of it nothing more inviting than a corridor of dark wet rock, as welcoming as a mine. Twas at least straight, ankle deep with water, the end of which beckoned with a lambency of pale light. Once again the trees were filling with whispers, so I entered the cavity. Wading at a stoop, I made my way toward the soft illumination. I stepped up out of the water into a large, dry, domed chamber that contained at its centre a stone plinth upon which was skewered the middle finger from a human corpse. This had been lit in the manner of a candle to provide a somewhat lurid yet remarkable luminance. Apart from this wizened maypole of a torch the chamber appeared empty. Though not for long. Soon the dome was chorused with whispers anew.

"See how our finger fair doth lick the air to light thine own peril. Do we not have skin dark and rough as oak?

Eyes black as night? Our vestures contain not a single stitch, so seamless is a shadow. Yet are we not thee, atavistic to a tee? Are we not entirely illuminated by sin? Hast thou not been summoned by the finger of a hanged man?"

The crackling tongue of flame licked each whisper, dialling sails of shadow over the ceiling.

"Is it not proper for a hill to contain an inclination? Poor little faery lost and found, snatched by whispers neath the ground. Am I not liken to thee? A faery up a tree. Though this one be sticky as bluebell gum."

Then did the whispers end. All twas heard was crackle of flame, lick of water, stir of air. With some haste I left the chamber, wading along the tunnel to the iron door only to discover it locked. Again I doused it with water. This time however it could not be persuaded to open. This time was no provision whispered. This time was I trapped.

Returning to the chamber, I decided to rest awhile to take stock of my situation. The entire temperament of this mischief was suspiciously familiar. That in itself is a common deception as never was one so well snared than by oneself. There's no doubting this was faery business. The chamber was dry, well lit. I decided to remove my coat to conduct a thorough check of my entire belongings. Everything appeared in good order. After clearing my thoughts with white snuff, I knelt on my coat to take a meal of scarlet mushrooms marinated with fish oil, washed away with violet wine. I keep a number of these tiny supplies within my coat's embroidered lining. Twas then I unstrung the purse given by Hatat. Removing the jewelled twine I proceeded to dangle it at arm's length as though I were fishing with the stones as bait. It then began of its own volition to rotate widdyshanks in a violent manner. Thus spinning did then the tourmaline appear to glow. Simultaneously did the flame upon the finger visibly wither. Twas an odd concurrence. Then with rigorous inclinations did the gems pull the twine with a pike's ferocity upward toward the dome's centre. Had I not had such a firm grip I swear the charm would be lost. With this divination firm set the tourmaline began to burn intensely as the human candle continued to diminish. Eventually, with the finger twice snuffed was the stone full blazed. Easing the upward strain on my arm the twine remained suspended in air, lighting the chasm with its miniature floating moon. Gathering my belongings and fastening my coat I had little choice but to fly into the concavity to retrieve my amulet and hopefully discover why twas thus beckoned.

I lifted into the air, bellowing upward with me a torrent of dust. A moment later was I hovered above the extinguished finger at the summit of the vault which disclosed a tiny elliptical niche leading to a narrow vent. Twas now obvious why the candle burnt so well without suffocation. Twas pointing all the while to a natural chimney. Whether this aperture could be safely navigated appeared dubious. Twas a tiny flue, coated with human soot. Not an appealing prospect. What's more, were it in any way to narrow twould be impassable. More immediately, for me to stand any chance at all of escaping thus, twould be prudent to shed the cumbrance of my coat. This done, I proceeded to reel in the suspended twine around its middle. Grabbing the amber I then towed the tethered stones and coat behind me into the vent.

Initially the shaft exited the chamber vertically. The luminous tourmaline, though somewhat diminished, was still able to brighten my prospective bolt-hole. Before long I hap'd upon a curious junction comprised of seven tunnels. Luck had so far kept the dimensions within the shaft fairly even. Though this was a game fast boiling out of humour. What's more, with the tourmaline now faded to little more than a pale glint, the way ahead loomed double dark. Twould I imagine be expedient, if one were swallowed, to make thyself as disagreeable as possible. On the other hand twould be cantankerous in the extreme to quarrel with a rock. This being so, did I choose the middle ground. Six is after all a number that encourages directness. Thus did I now find myself squeezed into the sixth tunnel from the left, crawling more in a horizontal direction than vertical, if gravity and exertion be fair indicators in what was now the blackest of worlds. At one point the new shaft dangerously funnelled. I was momentarily faced with the unpleasant prospect of attempting to reverse. I did however manage to wriggle through what turned out to be a narrow-toothed gap, taking the greatest of care not to impale anything of value. Once this hurdle had been breached, however, the tunnel thankfully widened into a more acceptable aperture. How long did I crawl? Tis difficult to say. Though it felt the best part of this entire journey was thus spent, squeezed to a pinch and powdered black. Then, abruptly as doth any shock introduce itself in this world did I round a corner into the wondrous lure of daylight.

Whilst entombed within the matrix of this hill did I consider the net that so deceptively entangled Mr Grimjaw. Doth not now the two of us twitch as doth a fly in a web? In his case tis dupery so well wove into cyclic fate that he remains in the skilfully veneered cell of his home, blissfully unaware. There he sits. Waylaid by eternal return, free from the spectres of a more linear inclination. Or is he? Doth not the wheel require a road? Through whose eye doth the universe eventually present itself? Surely tis only a pinch of perception required to navigate so short a distance as one's life. Both Boggles and Bugaboos doth jiggery-pokery cast. Yet do we not go round to round to merry ourselves or giddy our spirits? This hill hath stood my logic on end. If a weasel were to ponder the ocean, and a fish the runnel neath a hedge, twould be reckoned to contain significance, though twould benefit neither. Marry an abstraction and thou shalt fill thy days with distresses, if consummation by reason be thy desire. Tis a thought twould bite its own ankle in such a place as this, staring into the darkness of this world, white as a blinded eye.

Were I fresh born with wits enough to discern my first entrance here, no better surprised would I be as now. Were I to drink from a gong or pray to grass, this grim-faced enmity could not have been more unexpectedly resolved. I was now staring into a wide cold shaft. Twas no doubt a man-made well, plummeting into the drowned belly of the hill. Looking up twas like the spinal trunk of a mythic worm that doth swallow the day complete. Twas a massive bore-hole with shelves of rough stone trellised in light. Pinched between two bricks I balanced on a pressed step of crumbling mortar, peering down into a quicksilver of dark echoes. The rim was no further above my head as tis from the bottom to the top of thy home.

How faintly doth a child sob in this world? Why tis no more than doth a tear increase an ocean. Yet distinctly could I hear a child weeping. Tis a slippery place for sounds. Evasive. Difficult to pin-point any source juggled so. Yet there it was. Faint heard. Was it sourced from outside the well or within? I was close enough to the top for it to have been either. However, the more I listened the more persuaded was I that the sobbing was coming from below. Such faint distresses. Leapt I then into the blue-rimmed cauldron of the serpent's eye, full of apprehensions at having part broken the vow made to my grandmother. Flying visible within the confines of an enclosed space is not considered a breach of faith, for it involves little if any risk. But wells are by nature jittery places, haunted with wishes cast in tokens deep. Tis an unforgiving eye that stares up at the world. As I descended, the weeping was more fitful. I slowed my approach. Though unable to see the water I could hear it moved. I was now emitting so much flightlight that my reflection cast a white scribble over the face of the approaching pool. Suddenly, within the circumambience of my halo did I embrace a small girl, clutching a doll, submerged into the cold shadowy water to her chest.

Twas a shock to see so small a child in so relentless a place. Out of reach, though close as possible to her distressed soul did I now hover. Moving gently to and fro, never did her eyes blink or her gaze wander as she watched me with great intent. Tis confirmation she is still alert. despite her ill-fortune. Intermittent were her sobs, snatching the damp air in fretful breaths. She uttered not a single word. Clutching her doll as though twere her soul. I cautiously advanced, thus in my light's lure was I better able to measure her condition. She was obviously fatigued. I flew closer, confident her grip on the doll would not be relinquished at any cost. Unperturbed by my presence I believe her ordeal was such that her soul was beginning to succumb to her distresses. There is a point when we cease to call outwardly for help, listening instead for an answer from within to comfort our hopelessness. Twas such a time with her. Shivering in her dejection I flew yet closer still, more determined than ever to be of some assistance. Reaching out I cautiously stroked her nose. Immediately I retreated, unsure of her reaction. Gripping the doll tighter than ever did her stare remain fixed and her sobbing, though gentle, uneased. I re-approached and – risking all – gently kissed her nose. Again I retreated, but not as far as before. As I approached a third time, her weeping gradually lessened. Hovering no more than an arm's length from her face did she fix me most earnestly in her gaze. Her distresses continued to ease. Apart from the dripping of water and wing's whispers, was the well now quiet. Then, almost inaudibly, she asked me for help. Placing a forefinger over my lips as to beckon a hush, I gestured I intended to leave the well, hoping she would interpret this as an attempt to find assistance and not abandonment. With some misgivings I began my reluctant ascent out of the darkness, knowing that in order to effect any hope of an escape for her I would have to summon human help.

Curse on slate, sealed in lead, this well thy saint conceals a head. Serve thy snakes cast o'er the sea, the roots of trees doth search for thee. So it is with a well that misfortune can lose its 'mis', thus fortune be. This being so, did the sounds of approaching voices make me swift plummet back to the child's side. As a well doth two eyes contain or a spinning coin both life and death, did not I now find myself in more danger than the girl. Fretful at the approaching shouts from the wood above, spinning ever louder down the stone shaft, did my search for concealment become increasingly panicked. The child watched as I speedily scoured the rounded wall for a hole large enough to hide in. Were I stealing milk from a hare no quicker could I have dashed within this maledictive hill. Just then did she beckon me to her side. I flew over. We both looked up, as a man shouted close by. We stared at one another.

"Quick, in here." Releasing her grip upon that which she prized most revealed a neat portal in the middle of the doll's back wide enough for me to crawl through. "Quick!" And with the voices almost upon us I leapt inside, behind me swift her hand sealing our pact so speedily sought.

Tis best beware if fate doth sideways glance at thee, for no more fickle a mistress can there be. Thus was I now juggled within the hollow of this bosom, though not too rudely, for no better loved is a child by a mother as this doll by this child. Though unable to see, twas possible to judge from the conversations that a rope was lowered, having been secured to the winch above. Down this did slide a man, pitched at length into the trend of our shadows. Having steadied himself close, was he then tied off above. Eventually did he knot a second rope about the child. Then were we fished up into the vertical by other men. Once raised aloft, were we suspended within the flawed bell of the hill. Children are no less likely to betray a confidence as would their parents, though perhaps more keen to secure pacts pleasing the wonderment of their imagination, rather than any other greed. Thus are we all so finely balanced, dangling on a string.

Tis time now to elaborate upon this turn of events with the assistance of hindsight. It spins out thus. The two children, Vivien and her brother, were playing near the well, situated in a small clearing at the edge of a wooded hill, about a mile from their home. Their cottage belonging to a small tenancy of working families secured to a landed estate. The children had spent the morning dabbling on the wood's edge. By the time they reached the well, however, the pitch of a niggling dispute had escalated into a fight. In a fit of pique Jack abruptly threw his sister's beloved doll into the well. In a passionate lunge to save her most prized of possessions, Vivien lost her footing, promptly following her keepsake into the cauldron's belly, her fading scream sending Jack on a tearful dash for help. Twas in truth a terrible fall, though not entirely pitiless. Twas good fortune not to strike the stones as she fell, thus entering the deep water with wits enough to re-surface. Even so, she was completely shocked, thrashing round the black pool for an unseen life-line. Desperately clinging to the wall for a pinch of stone with which to support her threatened life. Combing the slimed bricks with her chilled fingers was her earnest fumbling mercifully rewarded, for below the water line her frantic legs had stumbled upon a dislodged stone, swivelled out far enough upon which to perch. As favours fair in three doth fly was she then reunited with her doll floating near. Thus twas we met, whilst unbeknown to us Jack was returning close with five men from the estate. So are we now returned to our present course.

Not for a second during the entire rescue and her subsequent revival did Vivien release her grip upon the doll. Twas obviously such a comfort to her shaken soul that twas an embrace considered by all as necessary. By and by was she serenaded with affections and assurances into a small bedroom. Eventually was she left alone to rest. Then and only then did she relinquish her hold upon the beleaguered doll allowing me to exit. Thus was I better able to take stock of my situation. Though somewhat tumbled was I otherwise well kept. Peering into the garden from a floor level window could Vivien see her father and brother. She assumed her mother to be downstairs tending her sister. Thus was her entire ordeal then re-enacted, as I ate a snack of vervain and hemlock, perched on the console of a tall brass oil lamp.

Tis true a house be larger than a doll, though never was I so ill-fitted in my entire journey to any place as I was this building. Sensing my unease did Vivien beg me stay till night. I flew to the window. Peeping round was I comforted to see a relentless crest of woodwave consuming the entire horizon close by. Just then did her mother begin to climb the stairs.

"Quick, Mum's bringing Rebecca to bed. Quick, into the doll."

Thus was I popped into the womb yet again. Vivien leapt into bed, thrusting the doll beneath the sheets as her mother entered the room.

"You alright my girl?"

"Yes, Mama."

"Where be that doll o' yourn?"

"Under here."

"That old thing nearly cost you your life. It's about time you were rid of it. It's years old."

We were both made increasingly uneasy by the path of this conversation, though twas gently spoken rather than abrupt. Once again was Vivien's grip intensified, pushing the skin of her arm into the hole on the dolls' back.

"Big girl like you shouldn't need a doll."

At which point was her sobbing renewed, much to the regret of all concerned.

"Alright, alright, alright. Come on. Stop crying. Come on now. Perhaps you could tell Rebecca a story 'bout your adventures in the wood and how you gave your Mum and Dad a fright. I'll be up again later. Night night."

Vivien wished her mother a tearful goodnight. Sitting within the increasing discomfort of this sealed chamber, I listened intent as she told her sister about a faery in the well. Twas a lengthy embellishment.

Then Jack entered the room. "You two still awake?"

"No, only me," replied Vivien.

He prepared himself for bed. "How you feelin' now?" he asked.

"Alright," came the whispered reply.

"Scared the life out o' me." There was a minute's silence. "Anyway it's late, time you were asleep. Night."

"Night, Jack."

Thus did the world fall steadily quiet, though increasingly uncomfortable due to the heat and lack of air within the doll. Thus could a leaf its roots discover, was I captivated at such length. Still did I wait, baked within the doll like a wicca's curse. It became worryingly obvious from the rhythm of Vivien's breathing that she may be cast to sleep, speedily dispatched no doubt by the exhaustion of her ordeals. I pushed on her arm to no avail. Twas becoming fast perilous for me, suffocated so. Twas enough to make a dressmaker spit thrice. Thus threatened was I left little choice but to resort to arms. Curse the fish, curse the bell, curse the hill, curse to hell. I drew my dagger. Place a pebble on thine eye, place a coin when thee die, fill with hair an egg clean blown, Thimblestar returneth home. Then did I thrust the dagger into the child's arm, flinching her dreams enough to mercifully dislodge the stifling embrace. She turned, tumbling the doll onto the mattress, thankfully exposing the exit. Though roughly gambolled did I leap to my freedom. I crawled from the bed and ran to the window. Twas well open for a small room with three children. I looked out. No need to risk a flight, the wall of the cottage was well netted with rose twine. I glanced back. Vivien was fast asleep, consigning her day to dreams, where no doubt soon enough my brief presence in her life will abide eternal.

## 27

Imagination doth a corner stone to magick make. Tis a commodity of childhood married to their wonderment. A realm of possibilities endless. Though tis tempered by a logic on the make. Tis a world where a faery though discovered remains hidden. Tis a world where an ocean doth contain a pinch of salt. Thus tis our revelations are better suited to children. When I was a child (though tis not the same for us) my mother would lull me to rest with this tiny rhyme:

"Between the autumn and the spring

swallows do a curious thing.

They fly beneath the waves to sleep

whilst up above the snows lie deep."

Thus were I to fly in an iron kettle could I be no quicker or safer despatched toward the great custodian of my domain as I saddled the nape of a passing hedgehog. Thus was I wobbled and scurried along the track's edge, past the sleeping cottages, down the side of a field as it swerved neath the hem of the great wood. The black of the sky and the white of the stars were soon stroked by beechy fingers long. Their ancient joints creaking in the night air o'er our heads as doth the fingers of an enchantress at her spinet. So it is we lovers all are lured. Soon was the moon well hid neath the puzzle of these branches. Tis true the wood be wild and dangerous but these are familiarities all. The great sweat of this place fixing my nostrils with hope renewed.

Hedgehogs often stop unexpectedly to snout the air. Tis always abrupt and unannounced. Passengers unprepared for this eventuality will most certainly be tumbled. Then were we immediately halted neath a ripple of roots in the scoop of a black lane where the cooking of this night was savoured through broomback's crooked snout. Without warning he slowly rolled himself up into a burden for any potential destroyer. I was unseated but unhurt. I leapt from the track into the fracture of a root midway up a steep bank. The cause for this evasion soon came snuffling through the night air along the lane. A badger. The bulk of its body trundled in the usual determined fashion. Tis an omen for sure. Gather thy news for thee to choose, cast o'er the world in twos, beware lest ravens search thee out, black thy wing, black thy snout. Thus has my beginning met itself. The badger pays little attention to the hedgehog, brushing the prickled dumpling of its rolled body with the toughened ball of its blacksnout before crashing out of view through a hole in the hedge on the far side of the lane. Tis a brief inspection that leaves me decided to remain secured amongst the roots where I lay in wait for the sun.

## 28

"Antelope, goat, ox or horse, serpent, fish, oryx, force thy alicorn gainst the tree, fear of death shall set thee free, yet virtue's odour destroy thy fabulous soul."

Thus was I awoken from shallow slumbers by this strange chant.

"My name be Jankin Galipot and cradled in my roots be thee. Tis fair to say this hill's my home, gripped beneath this tree. See."

Turning was I amazed to find a small door opened, revealing a bright tidy stairwell spiralling downward neath the roots into the bank. Tis a faery's encouragement to find so neat and well-kept an entrance.

"Welcome, welcome, welcome thee. Step in. Thou'll find me neath the tree."

Descending the neat uncluttered steps did my snout begin to percolate aromas both sourish and sugared. Twas an inviting breath of fumes.

"Spatter, splutter, spill and squirt, these are the names of my kettles. Pewter, iron, silver, gold, the family of their metals."

Thus did Jankin open the door to his magnificent kitchen and introduce himself.

"My name be Jankin Galipot, stood stoutly as you see, stupendous be my kitchens, gigantic neath this tree."

They certainly were very large. The ceilings being most spectacularly vaulted with massive roots, wild and coloured as the hair of a spriggan. Though twas strange to see so large a place contain so little. Just the four enormous kettles and an immense cauldron.

"These kettles contain the power of kings, white, crimson, black and blue. This cauldron be a griffin's eye where things that bubble see through years. Where things that pop dispel the blackest plots. Tis all one needs to summon deeds."

Twas a strange kitchen and Mr Galipot something of an oddity. Physically he was divided into three distinct portions. The largest of these was a very rotund body wrapped within a faded yellow jerkin. An enormous white collar opened to reveal a thin wry neck. This in turn supported a diminutive grey-skinned head. Twas so small that if his body were a 'naught' twould be no bigger than a full stop by comparison. From this dot of a poll sprouted a feathery white beard, the speck of a nose and two white dashed eyes. This outlandish mix of features was fashioned to the eccentric by token of their being clamped twixt the largest ears I'd ever seen. Were Mr Galipot's head and body silhouetted twould appear as a goat moth sat upon the moon with its wings apart. Both peculiarities were supported by substantial 'V'-shaped legs, stout at the thigh, dainty at the ankle, o'er which were stretched blue stockings pocketed into silver shoes.

"Allow me to introduce my brother. Goggie Bobadil."

Bowing low did Jankin move to one side, thus formally presenting me to the dignitary of a... blank space.

"Bobadil is wonder-working, thus difficult to see. He doth stoop like a question mark and roll on the ball of his foot. He is less likely to be noticed than most, on account of his sailing to Persia aboard the ark. He has asked me to extend his greetings. I was always the more enthusiastic concerning words. Thus it is I speak for two. I know what thou art mulling. Is Mr Galipot minkin, elf or chit? Mr Galipot be none of these. For Mr Galipot and Mr Bobadil have awaited in these kitchens, for more years than there be ghosts, the final ingredient to accomplish the desires of every wisdom. Thus tis you were awoken by the chant that summons... unicorns."

I was gestured to a table and told to make myself comfortable. Long ceramic ovens glowed in the dark. The kettles brewed, the cauldron spat.

"These doth chitter-chat of rocs, basilisks, hippogriffs, wyverns galore. Firedrakes boiled mightiest of all. Yet are these denied that which the unicorn alone can find. Tis true they may be summoned by the call of this hall. Yet are they barred by the might of our lintel. Only the unicorn can make the two turn three, thus revolving stone to gold."

Twas elfin alchemy for sure, but Mr Galipot was like no elf I'd ever seen. As for Mr Bobadil twas impossible to say.

"Tis time to eat, thus time to cheat the simplest hunger of all."

I was then presented a large dish made of frogs-glass, filled with the faery delicacy of scarlet berries soaked in dogrose syrup.

"Now thy stomach should thee fill, for soon thy soul shall we chill."

Reaching for my bow, which lay on the table, was I reassured by an anxious host that my welcome would be honoured.

"There be no dangers here for thee, lest kindness kill beneath this tree. Leave thy weapon, eat thy food. For what nearly was we often miss by fate as fine as the edge of a whispered word. Eat and listen whilst a tale I tell.

"On the far side of this hill spriggans there be. As well as we doth thou know the malice in their black hearts. Their notoriety for pursuing mischief at any cost. It appears that most recent did a victim they lure into their dread chamber, where imprisoned for life would the unfortunate prey satisfy her captors' pitiless lusts for torment. Now, it seems that their domain both heartless and cruel, free of any remorse regarding another's distress, was itself victim to a number of vicious assaults by a fearsome hawk. Spriggans are extremely evasive, as many an unwitting victim has discovered to their cost. Yet could this hawk detect their every movement, killing them at will. Then of a sudden, much to their relief, was the said bird discovered on the bank of a river, done to death, slain by an arrow poisoned, faery-flighted. Twas then spun out that the archer responsible for this favourable turn of events was none other than their victim fresh entombed. As a consequence of their law, not compassion, they were obliged to release their prisoner to repay the debt. Thus twas she was allowed to escape their wicked designs."

Jankin was right. Though warmed by the splendid food did now my blood run cold to learn that my life had been spared such torments by none other than the one I'd killed. Thus tis are we victims all.

"There be dandelion wine in the flask and butter-rattle neath this lid of oak. Maybe twould be best for thee to rest a day or two to contemplate the mix of it."

I was pointed in the direction of a small enclosure neath the oven where Mr Galipot and presumably his elusive brother had their beds. Twas far too warm a repository for a faery to sleep in. Mr Galipot apologised. I was then led to a cooler hold in which to rest. A small cubicle with broad wooden shelves. Twas ideally clean in which to dream. Outside twould no doubt soon be light. Yet within the world of Mr Galipot and Mr Bobadil did the scry of their eye find shadows a fair space in which to await all that had been summoned thus.

## 30

"Darkle, flicker, glimmer, gloom, there dreams a faery in this room. Half-light, twilight, light turned dark, there be no sun in here to mark the passing of our days."

Thus was I unbedded from a sleep separated the night long by unwelcome images.

"Tis a mark of our pedigree to thus insure the dark reveals to those in need all that is to see. Therefore doth Mr G and Mr B Adjure thee to the Bodkin of our tongues. Here do we Conglobe the entirety of our design, even though the Dander of the Egyptian Foretime doth vanish Mr B like a Gibus. Here do we beckon both with the Hink of a chant. Here doth the Incension of our ovens Jounce our kettles. Here can the Ket of the Leavy shine as doth the Marybud for the Notionist. Here doth the Outfall of our kitchen Pour. Be it Quat or be it Relucent. Sennit thy hair, thus braiding the Tine of night. Unwanted be the Vapid or the Nantwit in so sacred a Xyst. Yaup thy days away, no heed will we pay, at this thy Zenith."

This was all too much for me. The continued chanting. The gloom and sweal of the kitchens. Twas too keen a reminder of my previous call within this hill. Unaware of my increasing urge to be underway, Mr Galipot continued.

"Our mother died of falling sickness. She was born in the hoof of a dead horse. Upon her death were we willed to cast her talisman into a lake of deepest water. Famed for her crampstones would she immerse the desired rings in a boil of oakgalls, cockroach eggs and powder of mothwing. Thrice blown, a rat-tailed horn would bless the soup. She had maroon skin and was pretty as a damsel fly."

Jankin quickly produced from beneath the table a large jar of dried moth eggs.

"Tis normal to soak these in a strain of tutsan, then plain bake the seeds into a dumbcake. Passed through a ring of gold can then the simple mix topple the staunchest defence of any virtue. Thus is the will the way. And tis thy will I know to be re-aquainted with thy intended course most vigorously. Worry not. For Mr Bobadil hath whispered into the ear of Mr Galipot concluding an argument this night long with the difficult yet invaluable Mr Melchior. Twas all plainly baked and pops out thus. From our doorway widdyshanks must be thy course till thou hast cleared this hill. All the lefts will be thy way to free thee of this place once and for all. Spriggans too. Twill course thee at length into the darkest wood. Yet truly is this thy best path."

Thanking Mr G and Mr B was I led to a lobby. Grasshopper legs of every shape and size hung from wooden pegs. These are a universal tool, usually traded by sprights, but fashioned because of their durability and diversity by all with wits to do so. At last the door was opened and by the bye was I released into the grace of lordswork, free at last from the confines this hill had inflicted. As fates in three doth manifest the world, tis hardly surprising such a trinity was expressed. Thus within the hill did I endure two opposites connected by the one.

## 31

Dialling a slow cincture away from the hill into a damp gully was the sun lowered and the air cooled. A ferned dell stepped deeper into the wood from a stone ledge. This led to a ravine, stitched with periwinkle, tickled by the trickle of a brook. With night approaching, the thought of having to secure myself so soon from the prying eyes of predators was almost too frustrating a burden to bear. Faeries see well enough in the dark. Concealed by the alchemy of elfin tea can we dash twixt the thickest forest on the blackest night without harm. We can hear and smell keener than most. Yet doth the dark hone a host of unknowns. Tis a disadvantage to be a visible stranger on uneven ground. Thus did I start, albeit reluctantly, to look for a shelter as the first drops of rain tapped the leaves. With the hill of the spriggans and Bobadils some way behind, was my disquiet with the present somewhat soothed. On all fours I scrambled over slippery stones and sticky clay into a cobwebbed veranda of dusty rock. Twas dirty but I was much relieved at its discovery, as soon the world without was submerged by a confluence of darkness and water, thrashing into the mud with violent splashes and plumes of drums. Thus did the earth begin to spill and slide into the chute of the night. Sheeting onto the trees in cascades of thunder did this disobedience inflame the dark as though day had flickered the air. A rat sloshed quickly along the balcony of greasy mud that doorstepped my hideaway. Ensnared within the storm's upheaval did a frenzy of wind clutter the clouds. All about was the wood draining the sky into its heart. Crouched inside my retreat did I watch this turmoil agitate the world the night long. Thus at length was the above seeped into the below. In such a place and time as this, tis wise to be alert, for when stormy-bark the cloudy-dark will weasels rip thy soul. Fortunately did the night pass with the former shouting loud evidence but the latter mercifully absent.

The morning arrived, subdued by the night's commotion, suitably mottled in an opalescent veil. I restrung my bow then brushed the dirt from my coat. A check on my belongings procured some small strips of dried cep, which were delicious to chew. I made my way carefully back into the ravine, mindful of the brook, now bewitched by the storm into a racing surge. Masked neath the bracken I advanced into the sinkage of trees. The day persisted in a drizzle. Twas best to distance myself as far and quick as possible from the ranty water as its clamour hid all else. Eager to amend for lost time I dashed under cover of the ferns till near exhausted. Then did I discover a mighty rock risen from the sorrel and buckthorn. It jutted out over a pit of nettles and hung as doth the epic protuberance of a hob's nose over his beard. Twas a massive block, unusual not only of shape but colour too. How this tower came to fracture the woodland in so remote a place was an unapproachable question. Outstretched above the trench was the aim of its toppled crest aligned to the forest's ancient heart. The current of the entire situation a mixture of solemnity and avoidance. Here was the magick of oldtime dormant but far from exhausted.

# 32

My father suffered the affections of persistent magick. Thus twas, his heart displayed the unpredictability of a kaleidoscope. His temperament revolved by the aspect of the hour. Skin green as deathcap. Eyes, sulphur yellow. Slept on the bed of a mermaid's purse, traded from antiquity. Would suck the eye of a snake-fly or leg of a wasp. Could sunder a devil's darning needle with a single blow from his pikestaff. Best avoided when the nights were milky. Thus twas we traded our devotions with a deficiency of familiarity. Wore quilts of speckled yellow and mottled umber. Endured enlightenment offered by fluids fit to poison all else. Wore hats of pupae and masks fashioned from bugs. Could charm the legs off a spider 'fore toasting the delicacy of its head. Concealed his wisdoms within the animosity of an earthenware maze. A labyrinth baked into the roots of an oak by those whose dust irritated the nose of a bear. Within it, did the wraiths of a thousand futures navigate a whisper's thread into his estranged heart. Twas a place where the unwelcome were exhausted of power. If one were to escape it and drown twould be considered fortunate. Twas said by my uncle that father's knowledge of astrology was spellbinding. I remember only the spice of his breath as buttercup broth and root of witchbell. Could with willow save thy soul from marsh or pool. No saint was he, but could lead a wolf by the stone of its heart or the stump of its head. Kept two trout in the well of his mirror. For tis a truth the best gold be smelted in heaven to interrupt the nights. Were not the fondest rubies plucked from the holly? Thus twas his wealth be attained by so simple an alchemy. Yet could he reduce any entirety to dust by a trickster's art.

"Trance thy days, trance thy nights, thus tis the oracle of thy head delivers thee delights. Darkness white invokes the chase, a dainty dish doth follow. Entranced by dance, deceive the sorrow of the morrow."

Twas my father's art of avoiding any unnecessary experience. Destroy a toad, destroy thy mother. So was I often rebuked.

Finally was he butchered by a black dog on a careless night of the second month. Eaten alive, according to my mother. Disappeared into the labyrinth of its entrails. Hastily did we track the killer and boil its urine, though ne'er a trace was found. So tis, akin to this stone, he'll never disfigure. Vanished with the corpus of his name intact.

Tis but worldswork.

## 33

The fallen stone was strewn with abandoned snail shells, their succulent cargoes long removed. Tiny spirals coupled to grooves motifed its ageless face with a curious rugosity. Rendered almost undetectable by hollows of rain water were diminutive gouged shapes of feet and hands. Even more speculative were the dishes of silver and glass. No doubt disrupted by rain were these dainty vessels spilt, tipped and strewn. A dark rouge of fire dabbed at random. Surely, in such a place might Hatat's jewelled twine work to some advantage. Making my way toward the end of the promontory did I pass a scattering of bird bones. Twas a blunt reminder of how vulnerable a projection this was. Yet did it feel safe, though totally open. Even so, are not the best traps ensconced by deception. Accordingly were my weapons to hand. At its brink the stone tongue formed a cusp, rubbled with chalky nodules. The entire bulk jutted into the morning's windless saturation. Here was the vicinity's quiescence tasted neat. Twas though the stone slumbered with the wood politely hushed. More a repose than a deathliness. Returning toward the disrupted foundations, I stopped once again at the strewn dishes. Here was a large pool collected into the rock. Sitting at its edge did I remove Hatat's twine from its purse, dangling it at arm's length above the water. A procedure identical to that used in the spriggans' dread chamber. This time however was the result entirely negative. The suspended charm as motionless as the hushed forest. Twas though the world was locked.

Yet was there evidence all about me that this was a place

of some activity. By whom or what remained a mystery. I decided to recover my jewelled twine and sojourn till night. Perhaps darkness would uncover a portion of this unknown. But now was I dismayed by the reluctance of my amulet to move. No amount of force could persuade it from its stubborn suspension above the pool. It hung in the air as though its entirety had turned to stone. Twas completely rigid, fastened to the spot. As there was no thought of abandoning that which had been so solemnly offered, twas all I could do to sit and look at its puzzling petrifaction.

## 34

"Unenlightened are the inexact."

I turned to find a small crouched figure collecting the dishes.

"Unenlightened are the inexact." It repeated this upon recovering each dish. With a wading-bird's stoop did it pick about, crouched within a pink cloak. The beak of its lilac-skinned nose inclined continuous to the rock. A tree-creeper trapped in vestures would fit the bill of its make. Nor could it correct the curve of its posture. The rarity of its pinched legs suffocated by exaggerated socks. "No time to indoctrinate. Stone requires stone, else tis too late."

As it approached could I see its jacket brown, its breeches blue. Did the corpulence of its orange lips protrude as to kiss the air, rivalling the hooked combination of its nose and chin for length. A startling filament of yellow eyes bore out neath pouted lilac lids. Half capsized on crooked spindles was its bird-like gait squat to the crack of worn knees. Its entire pitch laboured well beyond a jig I suspected.

"Thou art a streak of rareness my pretty."

From beneath its cape did a finger poke, long as a wolf-spider's leg, the bud of its orange nail swollen from the digit like witch's-butter. Twas supported by the mismatch of its arm, a mere bump of muscle. Then did it point to my jewelled twine.

"Thy talisman is truly snatched. Stone requires stone to get thee home. This tongue doth speak well enough when spoken to. Though now the world be deafened by faltered choice to the wisdom of its voice. Once twas a science shared by all, from giants to the blessed small. Tis now a reluctant mystery, capsized midst the drowning of stars. There's little relief from ignorance in this world's orbit. Tis no fault of thine own that divination via this stone requires realistic complexities. Else tis, a hedgehog might topple the moon."

Placing the dishes round the pool did it then pour oil into each from a small leather cask. They were then lit in turn.

"Now must ye will the gift away. If not truly done there must it stay till earth be fire and sun be ice."

The pace of proceedings rendered an instant harmony impossible. Desperately did an amendment I crave, denied by apprehensions.

"Think of thy hat. Tis simple as that."

So, did I think of it. For there it was, wizened in the quartz by spritish guile. Instantly did the gem begin to burn on the twine. Fierce white in a flash did it outshine the circle of oil. Then did it flicker red as an autumn berry. Finally was there a spark of fire as it vaporised. Turning to the bird-like figure did I hear a 'ploop' as the twine fell into the pool. I was gestured to retrieve it. Sure enough was the quartz vanished.

"Tas literally gone to earth. Tis a good sign. Small compensation for thy ignorance."

Pursing what remained did we make our way slowly along the stone.

"North, south, east, west, it matters not. For surely do we all of us end where headed."

## 35

"Such a one as thee would cautions endorse. Tis surety
for thy soul in this world's course. Thy talisman hath by a
simple laudation received approbation. Genuinely am I
underwriter to the deed. For tis by these deeds am I
known. Hence no name have I."

We walked some way in silence.

"A great rain this way comes. Doth not the sky contain
its footprint, the air its fragrance. This slab can trace a
breath between the seas. Were men to discover the
entirety of their loss would the cursed nature of their fate
be plain seen. Had not the world know their like twould
be better served. This way."

Near the footings of the obelisk a great upheaval of
stones, peppered vivid with moss, counted our way as we
descended a worn stair of pebbles into the monolith's
shadow. Beneath the vast balcony of its inclination was
the track curved to the step of a door.

"Dost thou like it? Traded for a spot of fire."

Twas an intriguing door, fashioned from a single fork
of bone.

"How cleverly doth it all in one contain posts, lintel,
cusp and key. Tis a wishbone. So, tis merry-thought in,
merry-thought out. Come."

At a stoop did I follow the elegantly-plucked steps of
my host into the darkness. Twas the blink of a hallway
'fore our entrance into a substantial domed chamber,
plastered with a daub of dried mud, embellished
spectacular with mosaics of snailshell.

"Tas the art of a weatherglass. How prettily doth the
snail conceal its flavour. Beautiful orange-browns,
yellows, golds, whites. Striped as the fondest sky.

Brindled as the richest tree."

A lamp of oil did whorl the colour by small enticements. Twas an offering fit to comfort many a need. Yet was the true glory of this grotto contained in its floor. A single bloom of moonlight.

"Tis a plate of pewter. Years back was it found within the wood then dragged to these foundations. Twas dull as a toad but right of shape and strength. Over the years hath our movements uncovered the abundance of its lustre. Tis a resplendent base upon which to perch."

Unsurprisingly did we sit to a meal of molluscs. This was complemented by bread that bit back, twas so hard. Declining the water did I chase this languid fare with a fire of spit and snuff, thus burning its tail for luck. Just then did an arrival shadow the door. Hopping into the stately dome was it swift followed by three others. Now was I sat with five birdlike figures. Twas fast taking on the aspect of an aviary. What's more, were these recent additions mantled ominously black.

## 36

"What am I telling thee? Twill not walk, increase by size or jeopardize immortality with an animal's frailty. Thus tis the ridiculous notions of men arrange this universe. Tis the powder of their stars to cosmetic the fool. They will discover precious little to their merit, for it is their stupidity that eclipses all. There is nothing told by them that cannot be undone."

The cloaked figures sat motionless neath the sermon's tirade.

"Listen. A great storm hath been dispatched to threaten our lives."

Sure enough had the rain returned. Its drumming peeled thunderous through the earth.

"Do not concern thyself with this sombre quartet. Tis their calling to mourn a demise. Thus tis their lives are whittled."

This was fast turning into imp's work, though was I glad to be thus cloistered, such was the storm's ferocity. A chilled wind poked the door. The flame trembled in our midst. Then was the entrance blasted, filling the dome's lung with cold air, extinguishing the flame. A raging conflagration struck the sky. A moment later were our feet covered with water. As there had been no furniture to obscure the floor's splendour were we soon immersed to our knees. Twas such a violent stir that with ease it plucked the chamber clean of its art. Uncannily did it suck and swirl as doth a snail. Then did the entire building shudder. Now was the water whisked chilled black to our waists. The dome jerked and jolted, rotating in a frenzy of lubricated stones. Finally did the storm's confederacy conspire such a tumult that the entire chamber was extricated with an immense judder from the earth as easily would a corkball from a mouth filled with port. So were we launched into the torrent's embrace.

By some miracle did the quake somersault the dome complete into a swollen river. Floated off at an alarming speed did I now find myself alone in the upturned receptacle. How twas I survived in its base when all else was tumbled into the abyss I know not. The entire catastrophe had taken so short a time to execute its impulsive nature could its agenda romance a second. My immediate concern now was keeping the spinning container afloat. Twas after all a mere mould of mud. Flight was not an attractive option. My coat was saturated to a weight. The night black as a spriggan's heart. Branches scratched and spun the vessel constant, coursed into the wood's embrace. Twas all I could do to sit tight in the mix of its belly midst a paste of shell and mud. Clutching the dish which had contained the oil did I make a pathetic attempt to bale myself out. Fortunately the rain ceased. Nevertheless was the river's excitable state a commotion of destructiveness. Were one saddled to a demon bound for hell twould be no more furious. Boiled and roared in a frantic streak. Spun toplike in the ferment. Crashed, kicked. Nor did the tempest look fit to moderate. Overhead, the trees' convulsions raced by. Then did the river wind into a screw of brown milk through a funnel of rocks. Instantly, the vessel cracked. Water gushed into its hold. I instinctively leapt for life, clearing the capsized dome with not a second to spare as it folded into the deep turmoil. A moment later was I hooked yet again in the branches of a tree.

How prettily doth the dainty dance when cruellest fate

forgoes thy company. For then tis time to offer thanks, rejoicing in thy soul's reluctance to count the jig in total.

## 37

Someone called. Slowly was the river's impatience whispered into a dreamy insubstantiality. Someone called. The night tranced into vaporous fancies. Someone called.

"What am I telling thee?"

So was my head a vaguery of fleeting whispers.

Again someone called. "What am I telling thee?"

Thus tis the night can face both ways and thy head be double tongued.

"Wake up. Snail and snuff hath conspired a delirium. Wake up."

So was I conveyed from an intoxication so implicit that I was now in a fever of befuddlement. Tis dangerous stuff, ground white to snuff. Though poor Mr Snail with a flame on his tail could still his course not quicken. So was a fire suspended in my head. Nor were the embers yet doused. My birdlike host, one minute kind, the next grotesque. The mosaic dome fleeting twixt constellations of warm colour and a cold arc of space teeming with malicious eyes. The pewter floor, a drowning pool of mercury. At length did I become more settled. The rigors eased. My host, less threatening, more comforting. The chamber less divisive.

"Thou hast had a fit of agitations. No sooner were the molluscs vanished and thy snuff pinched did ye faint into a fidgety trance. Twas a terrible commotion of delirium, as though a great ferment had carried thee off."

Tis commonly said that one can further see from a tower's top than its bottom. So must ye risk a bat in the belfry to be a seer.

"Thou must tell me all, if tis to signify any relevance

by interpretation."

I was somewhat relieved to discover that the four cowled figures were consigned to my imagination. Though their significance was no less worrying. So was the night's work unspun by degrees.

"Have we not bounced this night as doth a pea neath a basin of tin to identify a plot? Tis certain as the toad doth quack or uncleanliness be purged by fire. Twitched in the leg, felt in the bone. A divination often savoured where the poppy burns brightest. Here, drink this. Tis curmi, made of barley. If ever a bottle contained a message tis this one."

Twas gold warm to chase the chills. At length was I relaxed into a more pleasant state, lulled finally to gentle sleep as doth a summer breeze the fidgety chick.

## 38

I was awoken by the oddest call of a song to a morning bright as charms. Light fired the open door to spill its brilliance cross the floor. My birdlike host was tapping a cane on the pewter, chiming the measure.

"Bring me a stork to keep off the fire,
A tall stork with glasses of wire,
Full of strong stories, a seasonal head,
A magical shape for maidens abed.
Bring me a stork that's not at all fussy,
Will nest in a cartwheel, pear or plum tree,
Is sung to by scholars assembled in classes,
Is not one for gathering together in masses."

He was repeating this over and over, walking anti-clockwise upon the dial of the minute.

"Beware my faery lest thee be found by those who dwell beneath the ground. For evil short is evil long, when what is right be all times wrong." Turning toward me did he then continue. "Tis good to see thee returned to a fairer aspect to serenade the morn. I have pondered the conundrum of thy dream till the mix be coagulated. So shall the curd of this treason float itself. This world will but by one truth be measured. Come."

I was gestured to follow him out of doors, back along the bank, up to the stone.

"No fair a morn could a crystal scry. Where hast thou travelled from? Where dost thou travel to? Where be this place in the balance of it?"

Thus was my entire quest unspun, bound as it was by

an oath never to fly visible in this world.

"Tis as I feared a half done thing. Half said, half dreamt. Spoken by me, seen by thee. Four figures wantonly summoned. The prediction perhaps of a storm or turmoil yet to come. Thy soul carried off by a force at once predictable, yet full of unknown terrors. For what is as water is, yet not? Float thee to the world's end it will. For do not the dead thirst for it? Tis their fate to be so misled as to necessitate the fool. Here on this stone, grey as fate itself, order can be restored. Thus tis the poisoned finger of improvidence can point the way."

Never was I so confused by such findings. Mr Stoop had been kind to a point, though now I felt his eagerness to relocate my path had vanished it the more. Unfastening my coat was I better able to check the stitchery of my inheritance. Its warren of small pockets revealing a modest tally of edible surprises. It appeared my effects were in good order. I then proceeded to arrange my arrows for inspection upon the stone. These were immediately pounced upon by my cloaked host.

"Six black figures, six black figures," he shouted. "See." Pointing to my arrows, tapping each with his cane. "Here be the measure of thy journey. For two more must ye loose till ye be found."

He remained the more convinced of our party as he mulled a mumble of propositions from the stoop of his form.

"Be patient. Be attentive to thy dreams. How else can a thought be replenished? Thou hast spent the night afloat the wildest of wheels. Taken to that which can be cleansed only by that which took thee. Tis no great advantage to survive a flood then drown in ignorance. Thou hast navigated a well-earned port from the muddy belly of thy boat."

Mr Stoop spoke elements of truth but they flickered as tiny stars in an otherwise lightless void. Twould require considerable skill to navigate by their design.

"Listen to the sextant of thy soul to decipher that which has been shown. Come."

The wood was brilliant lit as we promenaded the stone. The vaporous suffocation of the previous days evaporated. Twas my opinion that no greater fool was there than one who claimed all knowledge. For never was a life so misspent than by such vain imitation. Not so misguided but giddy as a mix of millet did the store of Mr Stoop's knowledge appear to rise half-baked. We were now halted at the rock pool where previously was seized my jewelled twine. Dishes of oil once again lay strewn in disarray.

"Look at these lamps. Tis by the sacrilege of birds they are scattered thus. Sometimes do I poison the water in this pool to kill such an ignorance. Then will I burn its bones into a morsel of soot. Never was a warning better writ."

Suddenly I was overcome by so great a desire to be underway that I decided there and then, forsaking all, to leap into the air and be gone.

"Not yet," Thus taken by the arm was I led further along the stone. "Tis right that what is half seen be also half hid. Such is the fickle nature of all truth lit by one sun. Do not be in too great a rush to seek thy invisibility. Tis plain the way ahead be fraught with dangers great. Yet that which has shown thee twice will show thee thrice. There be providence in a prism, wherever ye care to dangle it. I refer to thy amulet of course. Look."

Taking two steps backward into the shadow of my

host did I swift unsheathe my dagger, as a great bird appeared from the far trees, soaring toward us. Made nervous by the lack of cover was I swift assured by my host of its benevolent intent. A moment later was it alighted in our court. Mr Stoop then struck the stone three times with his cane. Bright eyes immediately replied, tapping the stone vigorously with the stout lance of its bill.

"Fear not, for is not the blush of thy crowns identical? Gingerknob, meet Mr Gingerknob. This one I feed a kinder diet than most. He has a partiality for ants. Thus tis we tap our talk to the small measure of its vocabulary. He has an honest coat, the green of which displays his kingdom well enough. He has an honest name too. Therefore he is to be trusted when all else is not. Wait."

Mr Stoop then struck the stone intermittently with a series of sharp clouts in a strange radial motion. Mr Green answered by scraping his beak criss-cross upon the stone as though t'were a quill before rapping a dab to conclude.

"Good, tis settled. Mr Viridis will fly thee by kind consent as far as he is able to the limit of his compass upon the course set for thee by Mr B and Mr G. No fair an outcome to our work can I aspire. I feel tis the best answer to thy impatience. Now be gone."

Quickly did I mount the transport to complement our eagerness. My host produced a length of cord from the pocket of his coat with which I fashioned a noose around the bird for security. Then, with a brief fare thee well, were we speedily launched off the stone, across the ditch and into the forest.

## 39

Turning did I watch intent as the monument rapidly receded neath freckles of leaflight. The waving figure of Mr S. wilting as doth a candle on a cake expiring its greeting. Soon were we swooped through vast turrets of wood. Then fired into looplight by our haste in the common turn. Sped into brilliance. Flight fondly remembered. Truly were my expectations now fairer faced. Though was I cautious to lie low, hid best as possible upon the bird's back, mindful of unseen menaces that doth bitter mix all things unguarded into the broil of their unsavoury soup. Even so, there be no better way to shorten a distance than this. For what be thy soul's delight other than flight? Soared twixt grizzled oak. Florid with a thousand complexions. Great shadows of copper cloud hovered. The world rushed into earthshine. Its luminance scintillating the eye beyond its horizon. Flight. Fairest of treasures. Measure thee then by this delight the earnestness of that vow which bound me to my grandmother's wish. Flight. When excitant wings purr thy body entire from a life of gravity into the animation of spirits. Elevated thus do we electric the filament of our body to such an extent we glow as doth the wayside worm. Flight. Where the purges of thy life evaporate into ether. Never have I missed it so. Glided cross the forest's breath into its darkest heart.

Now was the air grown cool. Chilled waves hovered our drift into a slow descent over a shrubbed thicket, onto a fallen hazel. Round about did willows and alder trip their frocks to the wind's drifted ground. Twas so peaceful a jig as to entice the greatest of smiles. Here was the cavernous plume of the wood most verdant. Mr Greencoat squat motionless on the toppled ruffle of bark. Twas a fond station for the like, with substantial debris from fore and aft permeating the air. Nevertheless was I both grateful and gracious. Thus did I extend all courtesies. Twas in turn reciprocated with a crimson nod. Then did he tap his talk upon the bark in threes. Twas brief but inexplicable. Though a measure of simple guesswork sized a fond farewell. Unfastening the twine did I roll it into a pocket. With a check of my bow did Mr Greencoat hop a turn facing right. He then struck the tree a deft blow with his beak, indicating a direction by so determined a point twas impossible to ignore. Birds navigate by that which spins us in the heavens. Tis therefore reckless to disregard such advice. Furthermore, I had noticed the colour of Mr G's beak. Grey. The colour of fate itself according to Mr Stoop. A coincidence best heeded. Using my bow did I rap the tree in turn, then point it as a recognition of his council to the chosen course. Thus indicated did Mr Green hop unceremoniously from the log into the air. So was he glided from my life into shadows, then vanished in an instant by merit of his art. So it is that souls do part.

## 40

Haste and style had now conspired to transport me a considerable distance. Though was the mile reduced to the inch in alleviating my frustrations by this journey's maze. Were I to throw an arrow or pick a gibbet would the half of it stay hid. Were those that know the road to hell disposed to pen a map, no better placed would I find my soul. For here was the forest's flux blistered into air. Poplar, ash, oak, willow. Fern, bracken, wort and tongue. Grass bug beaded, lichens blotched. Here did the meadowsweet and gooseberry wild it fond. Were the bramble to prick thy blood t'would contain the familiarity of a mother's kiss. Yet did I remain lost within this known world. Were I to sneeze or creak a chair would all roads cross to damn thy soul. This be a great and ancient forest cast in thousands over earth. Thus could its roots absorb the heavens even to a star. Its branches so numerous as to foil any evil disposed to fill our faith into a void. So it is this happy orbit tilts our heads. Yet am I for the want of it lost.

Party to the wisdom of Mr Green must I now make haste as doth the devil in the berry. Our brief encounter can a further profit turn, hid as poison blushed in fruit, forbidden yet desired. Here did creep and bristle blacksnag as doth the damp daglock, both snail and spider spun. Here did the tall grass shine, fly-infested. Here was the ground soft as slug's eggs wedged in pulp, the yellowear hankered. Making my way neath a net of bracken did I arrive at an extended clearing, a vast length of the wood sheared from left to right. Clambering up the nettled bank to discover the cause of so comprehensive an opening was I astounded to discover a broad mighty river stirred between the trees, slid to sunder this ancient world by its immensity. Was this the river so soundly shaped by snail and snuff? If so, was the reality far monstrous than any imagined. Thus is the greeting half the parting, head and tail but one.

"Ever east, ever straight, twixt two hills, templegate. Ever onward cross the world until ye find a river swirled with great divide between our Lords. Then ply thy fear a cautious haste, for nothing can divide thy flight from its purpose in this domain. As ill and good doth scurry for the profit, make us swift amends. Ever east, ever straight, twixt two hills, templegate."

So twas, my uncle's words first dispatched me into the world for elfin tea. It seems as though a thousand years hath passed since first I saw this river. Yet has it never failed to fill my soul with wondrous distresses. Big to thee, yet a sea to me, such are the proportions of its strength. Imagine. Flying ceaselessly through woodworld, hour upon hour, the storm of colours shadows in a constant flicker of movements magic, suddenly to be cast out as though from the walls of a sanctuary into a space where nothing of thy world exists. Out across the broad face of a mighty river, displacing the irreducible with a perilous profit wherein ye dare to find another. Thus summoned, must this strength then join by flight that which water mightily separated. For tis often the case that things be divided by none other than that which connects them. Even so, must ye dare by wing and prayer to cross the race of its drowned soul. Never did I fail but with trepidation to make from bank to blessed bank. Now, with wings bound by oaths, here I stand, facing the magnitude of its colossal slide toward a distant sea.

"Hath we by might disclosed a river to haunt thee with desires untold. Thus in shadows shown doth eternity beckon. Tis here, the dread face of thy soul's ambition."

Thus twas my father's words touched upon the unfathomable nature of water. Its immeasurable deathlessness.

"Tis what binds thee to the stars, my little button of a queen."

The science in the egg as he termed it.

Mother was less poetic. "I'm told tis in most things common. Yet would I never knowingly drink it or have it touch me. Shall I tell thee, my little hare, how the future beckons? Faceless as a turquoise ocean. Listen. Tis commonly believed that water can cleanse thee. Never was so large a lie spun in this world. Twill merely make thee wet or worse still, snuff thee out. For my part, I take it drowned with spice or not at all. You would do well never to trust it."

Grandmother on the other hand maintained that the true faith of alchemy was simplicity. "Thus tis the entire history of all things be fire and water. Alchemy is based not on artifice but goodwill. Listen close, my little spriggit. Truth is self-revealing. The art is to recognise it. Not paralyse it with ridiculous vocabulary. Thus tis, men were never good at these things. Alchemy is a science that simply measures truth to necessitate freedom. Water and fire will reveal nothing that isn't there."

Grandmother was of course a great alchemist. Hath not this story already revealed the measure by which I judge her words? My heart fondly stowed her benevolence as a credit to her advice. We loved one another very much.

When questioned, Grandfather said very little. Words and silence, as far as he was aware, never mixed. He was mindful that there was water in the world but, as far as he knew, it had not outstayed its welcome, yet.

If I was my mother's child, Winkleprimbell was certainly my father's. By such a token were her views inclined eccentric. "Shall I tell thee what I think of water, my quabble of insignificance? I think it measures the difference between thy father and mother."

My sister's preoccupations always denied any love that may have existed between us. Her heart was vacuous to displays of affection. Nevertheless, in other regards I was never denied. We were always respectful, always tolerant. In many ways, we mirrored the relationship of our parents. Even so, we were ever mindful, ready to avenge any injustice to the other from any quarter.

As daylight began to fail upon the face of the river, I became increasingly aware that I had spent the entire afternoon mesmerised in its reflective power. Undoubtedly did its movement contain my father's poetry. My mother's mistrust in its unbounded perpetuity. My Grandfather's undeniable observations. Even my sister's voice. Yet by far the brightest revelations were those of Grandmother. Her words had in turn resurrected the prediction of Mr Stoop's concerning Hatat's jewelled twine. That most treasured now of all possessions. For rightly had it twice rescued my mission. Therefore thrice might it reveal a course of action to save the day. Though mindful of its unpredictable qualities, did my soul keen measure the reclined shadow at river's days' end. I thought it prudent therefore to reside the night this side of the divide before attempting to uncover any solution by whatever means, enabling me to cross.

## 43

"If by shrew the scent of you
Should snatch his pippy-snout,
Or weasel, rat, mouse of field
By sniff should seek thee out,
Then fear not thy tiny soul
In world of tooth and claw,
For magic guards thee everclose
Both now and evermore."

So did I sing to comfort my soul's unease as the moon scribbled tender light across the water. When I was born my mother sang that song to me. So has it always reassured a need when needs be. So too had the day's geography counted the measure of my quest. For has not this river always marked it so? Though where upon its stretch I now lay remained unknown. For tis mightily spent by length of deed. Yet I feel assured that the journey be half done. For all time has this river divided our world. From where I lay in the split of a willow's bark I watched bats with fidgety flight scour the night air. Bats!

See a little leatherwing
Flitter, flicker flick,
Evading all its creditors,
That's a clever trick.

See a little leatherwing
Threaded heart of red,
Stealing all the bacon,
Ghosties in the bed.

See a little leatherwing
Flitter, flicker flick,
Best avoid its bloody teeth,
Nippy nicky lick.

So tis this night be hunted high and low by the like. Bow
and dagger kept to hand.

A tall jar made of moonglass containing bat's eyes sits
on a shelf in Mother's house. Tis said that cautiously
applied to a portion of words doth the mix reveal all that
by invisibility is hid. Mother often ate the dull little
pellets of filth, as did my father. I avoided them. As a
child I was given a potion to encourage flight that
contained bat's blood. No better able was I to fly by its
application, though was my soul close snuffed by the vile
concoction. Grandmother discovered later that my
reluctance was due to the tones of winter. Since then have
I declined the gifts of Mr Leatherwing.

As bats continued to nip the night, a full moon peeped
white as a goblin's eye over the river, winking at the
water between the black wood. Stirring silent inky
plumes of cloud. An owl called. Fluting dark woody
tones. If a man be a bird or a bird a man, surely would the
faction of its heart divulge a secret or two. So tis an owl's
call doth haunt with unseen promise. I have seen them
nailed to thy doors (much like a bat) to avert misfortune,
though never was the opposite more true. Father told me
that were a man to kill an owl, then pray as he might,
prey he will be. His scent perpendicular to the act, once
sniffed never lost by the blackwolf's vengeance. By all
means tipple the soup of its egg to cure an ill. But beware
ye who hath violated such a quietude, for no rest shall ye

find.

The fracture wherein I lay overhung the great interruption of water. Vague traces of daylight began to glass its surface with an opacity of owl-light. The farness of trees along the opposite bank cast a filmy curtain for the second act to commence. So was the night furtively dispersed along the river. Soon was its splendour glared into rippled flares of colour. Set once more to mirror the day. Set once more to glister the boundless fancies of thy soul's trance.

## 44

Have I not seen this world upside down? The night sky with starfish lit, the ground soft as a summer cloud. If the river has a mind for it, so do I. Perhaps we are not so unalike. Perhaps flight hath kept it misjudged. For now, face to face, a kinder aspect proclaims the hour. This day has found us the better judged. Even so, I descended the willow cautiously, for good and evil hath the balance of their souls unaltered by such a lesson. Hid beneath a shelf of grass on a small inlet I unpursed Hatat's amulet and inspected the remaining stones. Both tourmaline and amber sparkled keen as eyes. My worry was however that the charm was in some way compromised by the missing quartz. An omission that appeared to glare from the empty eyelet, foreboding what had been till then a fair morning. Once again was I sat with the jewelled twine at arm's length to fish the unknown. Gently did I lower it into the dark river, slowly submerging the stones. I took the precaution of binding the twine round my hand for fear of having my prize washed away, or snatched by some curious fish. No sooner were they sunk into the murky interiority were my apprehensions dispelled as the jewels began to glow in the depths, lit and rolled mesmeric as serpents' eyes. I gripped the cord intent, tracing their vague movements. Just then did a plume of shadow mute the water. Looking up, I expected to see cloud covering the sun, but there were none. Suddenly did the realisation that this darkness was below the surface of the river, not upon it, fill me with dread. Simultaneously was the cord gently jerked. Then to my consternation were the stones vanished. Immediately I pulled on the twine only to discover it snagged tight neath the waters. Repeatedly I jolted and tugged till near exhausted but no quarter was given. Fearful that I might be dragged from the bank and drowned I reluctantly eased my grip upon the twine. Determined however never to relinquish it at any cost to any force, seen or no, I looped it about a root for support. Then were my confusions stirred anew as my mind swirled with images from the dream experienced as a guest of Mr Stoop. This was fast turning into imp's work.

Time passed, swung fast. Thrice looped to the woodwork. Thus far was the day balanced even. So spent, was no additional force brought to bear from either side. Then to my relief did the twine slacken a slight, enabling me to further retrieve my prize. Again it eased allowing me to grab the more. Perhaps my foe was tiring. Perhaps, if knotted into stones or reeds, was the current undoing such a mix. I peered over the side into the water. The plume of dark lay shadowy neath the surface. Yet must it be more risen now as the first eyelet—the empty one—surfaced from the gloom. Encouraged did I haul the more, eager to secure its entirety, yet mindful of the unknown obstruction. Suddenly was I tranced by astonishment into a spellbound fumble of the cord. Scrambling to retrieve it did I stare in disbelief as the shadowiness surfaced the river next to the bank. Twas a face. Thy size. Man size. Yet twas not a man's. Or a woman's by that token. For its features were shaped from the very water itself. The skin a circulation of ripples in sparkled murmur. The eyes were closed. The mouth tight shut about the cord. Its entire complexion a wondrous flux. So fished, so caught. Lure the unknown, yet may ye find it. Mesmerised by the beauty of its watery countenance did I slacken the cord for fear of distressing it. Do not the pacified contain equal danger? Half submerged, I began to wonder if the delicate transparency of this glassy facade hid a darker art. Then, as though to answer the very query of my mind's focus, did the lucent eyes slowly open. Thus twas the fate of my jewels were exposed by the oddity of its stare, for having swallowed the stones were they now lit within its head as the brightest of eyes. So tis these gems do further see than me or thee. Tis but worldswork.

## 45

By what magic these tiny jewels conjure such startling combinations of providence I know not. Tis not faery in temperament. Transfixed by the floating face was I now stood at the river's edge. Tempted to touch the washed brilliance of so wondrous a ship did I ease my guard, reaching out. Gently did I pat the puddle of its enormous cheek, casting gorgeous loops cross its prism. Immediately was the slackened cord taken up as cautions on either side reversed our familiarity a pinch. Twas a fleeting mistrust, for not a moment later were we docked the closer still. Patience be not so much a virtue when the magic be half spun but of the absolute. Never were things made less well or worse still than by a rush. Never force the lock, for fear of breaking the key. So did the fisher and the fished remain for some considerable time.

Shadows dialled. I began to wonder how so strange a catch might solve the problem of my abeyance. No sooner thought, did the liquidity of its mouth begin to open. Soon did the well of its throat gape a face to the question. Deep within, unseen reaches of the river drenched dark. Cautiously, I began to haul the released twine from its mouth. Unsurprisingly were the remaining eyelets now noosed to little more than nothing. I continued pulling, unaware that the cord was about to expose a most startling addition. For attached to its end, inseparable as a full stop from a sentence, was a glassy bubble, which by gentle enticements I extricated from its throat onto the surface of the river, where it floated like a watery egg. This cord hath fed the strangest delivery yet. Twice more did I tug till the capsule was moored no more than a step's distance. There did it float elegant as any truth in this world. Transparent as finest glass was it plain seen that the cord's end remained settled in the pot of its boll. Once again held fast. No amount of force altered the issue. Securing my end of the twine to the root again did I then deliver my longbow though twere a bloodworm into both hands, with the thought of using it as a lever to free the cord. To my amazement did it pass clean through the wall of the vessel but refused to return. Imprisoned within the container this turn of events doth dress a more favourable idea. Least I have a notion for it, considering the benevolent nature of the gift. Surely then twould follow for me to follow. For without a word must the clue be seen. Or felt. Thus am I beckoned by the transparency of the token. The inclination therefore leads me to place a hand upon the sphere where amazement discovers its strange globosity fashioned from water, not glass. Fleshy, yielding to the touch. A springy, pressable membrane. Though was I cautious not to puncture its tender skin, mindful that what's admitted sits confined. Yet both bow and cord look happy enough in so shapely a ship. Surely there be room enough for one so favoured, plus a thousand faults therein. So must I commit to the task in hand. If there be an echo in it, surely doth it whisper of my soul's fortune neath a hawk. So twas I stepped from the question into the answer. From separability to coherence. From one moment's truth to the next, though they be scattered as stars.

## 46

Immured within the sphere was I now sailing upon the mighty river. Had not this entire journey been one of concealments? The hawk's egg. The girl's doll. Surely doth it follow that a bubble so delivered counts a perfect three. Though no sooner were we floated did the glassy popple abandon its transparency with a rubescent blush, obscuring the outerworld neath a screen red as earth. Now could nothing be seen with the exception of the cord's end, worming through the vessel wall. I bound it to my hand for fear of losing it. Though where it now led without, I knew not. Of one thing I was sure. No longer did it remain tethered to the root. Gently revolved and bobbed upon the divide. Jounced by strange compulsions.

Suddenly was the red screen lifted, revealing a world entirely of sky and water. Where was the land? Such a place as this might be careless with thy soul. Best be patient, though was there little choice, impounded in the pot. Then was the world vanished again. Concealed now by yellowness. Thus encircled did I sit to contemplate the mix of it. This be a colourful voyage indeed, and one that questions more than answers. For images that by snuff and snail fevered me at Mr Stoop's were curiously mollified by these immersions of colour. Such was their drift. Suddenly the yellowness vanished, uncovering a vast colonnade of trees looming close. Great comfort indeed for one so small. Though in the next instant was this too disappeared. Obscured this time by an albescence that resonated whiter than chalk. As fortunes fair in three doth fly, so must this be counted. Here was I reminded of

the egg most keenly. This be too white for just a
goodness. Then without warning was the bubble bumped
and rolled, tumbling me about. Instantly was the
membrane restored transparent. Revolved on a rainbow
of blown water spun the world anew. Haloed in a flare of
colour. Burnished over the membrane in a glassy fire.
Dazzling. Then.....

Pop! The globe vanished. I was left standing knee deep in
cold water, bow and cord in hand. I leapt to the bank.
Turning could I see yet again a rippled face risen in the
shallows. Twas identical to the countenance from which
was fished the bubble. For there be the oddity of its stare,
black-blue resin. But as I watched, the fire within the
jewelled eyes faded, the watery features dissolved.
Slipped from the spreading mouth was the twine sank
into the stilled pool. Twas apparent the liquidity of this
spirit had steered my ferry with the tow of twine. So tis
all things be threaded. I wound it in, thankful to have
witnessed such benevolence raised from darkness by the
merit of those tiny jewels. All three eyelets were now
vacant. Even so, have not these treasured tokens afforded
me safe keeping of my soul? Traded well as any sprite in
this world.

## 47

"Welcome. This be Olomonomolo's garden. Fairest in the land. Fast watered endlessly by this river's might, vexing the faithless to invent a faith overnight, to capture flight, or sail, as twas I saw thee come. Ferried well enough. Hid from the malice of birds and fish, both embraced, as indeed are we all, by the vanity of a mirror's call. Call, call all ye like. There be not a language yet devised that we cannot ignore. Or sing a song. Short or long. For this be Olomonomolo's golden garden. Prolong thy stay. For tis on the way ye have found us, busy as a buzzing wing. That's right, that's right. Peer up, peer round. Peer a peer without a bound, but found we will not be. Fear not the freckle of thy soul. For tis no unkindness or spiteful deed that keep us hid from thee. Tis more a need, a needy need, as needy as can be. Doth the pallor of my faithful skin blotch rotten when found out, so I tend to keep my skin within whilst my voice doth work without.

"Ah, Olomonomolo's garden. Sit. That's it, sit thee there. No better will ye find a chair, no matter who the lord. And lords there be up every tree on this side of the world. Stay a while. Imbibe the air, for familiarity with this chair will drive as doth a fracture through slate, twixt two hills, templegate. Thus framed the faithful fall, whilst the faithless measure the extremity of it. So I'm told. Though never did I trust a word so easy bought or sold. Now this garden, impossible to measure by any enthusiasm I'll wager, sits as a reminder to the transparency of words. There be not a single leaf in all the world contains a vowel. Yet doth it have much to say. Not all of it happy as the feeble-minded are so tickled to imagine. Tis tantrumed terrible by the season's rub. It harbours secrets in the black havoc of its roots where the unimaginable be whispered in shockingly familiar tones.

"Olomonomolo's garden. No fair an aspect will lure thy love. For no greater start in life there be. Thy ear, little dear, be well enthused for this rhetoric I can tell. Tis a gardener's art to thus impart the pattern of the now and then, yet again are we all entirely procured by nature's fancy that and yet ye may. Do not delay. Untie a confusion or two. So therein lies my art, to set apart the bunkum from wisdom. Though in truth should the two be separate from the start. So for those who dare without a care, or carry cares for the vagaries of merit or the abstractions of truth, can ye wash into no better a port.

"Olomonomolo's garden. No grand a ground has yet been found this world's length. For if there be a truth why waste it on the world? For does not the orbit of it rotate for vulgar consumption alone? Giddy in the worship of the self. Look about. Though this be the most secret of gardens no wall will ye see. For surely a wall raised to contain a secret also betrays it by merit of its existence. This be too great a wisdom to fall for so simple a trick. For tis thy soul alone can its borders see. Wherever ye travel from this place, will distance measure the memory of it. Or vice-versa. Any poet should tell thee a thing or two concerning its intent. Thus twas for every bloom a song be heard. Olomonomolo's garden then bids thee welcome as it bids thee farewell. Farewell."

## 48

Remember Mr Grimjaw? Every morning he awoke oblivious of the previous day's events. Enchanted into a cyclic fate of which he was unaware. Cursed some would say. Spellbound, literally. His memories stolen, his acquisitions removed. The yardsticks by which lives are measured. Thus twas I was swept from his keep. There is much treachery in this world to ebb thy faith in its true fortunes.

Not a day's walk from Olomonomolo's garden did I take shelter in the grace of a birch tree. That night was I visited by something unseen whispering within the branches.

"Inkblots, knucklebones, vapourish dead, water drowned silver, shape of a head. Dice or coins, dogstar lit, fall of a card, thy soul forfeit".

I listened intent. So muted were the words, so restless the tree.

"Once when the seasons were six, when the entirety was little more than a murmur, the warmth of sun and blood matched recent, was the first dream stolen. Twas placed beneath a mirror, guarded by a dog of bronze. So tis that more dreams than there be stars light the mirrors of this world. But when did a mirror ever show thee a truth? One requires only half an eye to see it, yet is the contrary the practice. Ye did well not to sleep in the garden that edges the river. For had thee not taken thy dreams elsewhere then none would ye have, both now or evermore. Accordingly are most things evil well turned out to seduce their prey. A pleasant aspect to lure a life away. Tis of course a wicked tenure. A devourer of dreams no less."

Mother once told me never to trust a voice without a head. By such a measure this be a dubious part of the world. For this be the second so unattached in less than a day. It continued thus:

"Water on stone, black dog dead, noseless face, hat on head. Red clay clinched, suffocate a mole, mortal shadow, lead blood bowl. Milk hath washed my bones well enough. Red ochre too. I be disposed to this tree some hundred years. Ne'er a dog has sniffed the west for me. Unaided by jug or cup, bead or coin. Mollified by the guiltless. Ne'er a mirror was turned for me. Hence the dead are reunited with their desires."

This voice doth sound uncannily like a sister's whisper. Strange too how earlier Olomonomolo's voice reminded me of Father. The night was aglow with moon lustre, sheeny leaves, glaring stars, yet cold as a goblin's heart. Secured in a split driven through the bark, I was safe enough. Warm too. Cocooned within my coat tighter than a snail in its shell. Or a meal in thy gut for that matter. Surely was I no less stirred. Shaken thus did it rattle on:

"Best count thy steps. Thou hast inherited the birthright of an exquisite coat as thou hast inherited thy ancestor's mizzle of memories. Much can be lost that cannot be reckoned. Yet this side of the river can count the cost quicker than a thorn winkle out thy dreams in a haunted garden. Olomonomolo would much rather I died in a cell of oak with a pan of meat, unburnt wheels beneath my feet. That I chewed the flesh with a pinch of salt before considering the question of my soul. So tis that so many waste what is given searching for that which is not. Best count thy steps if you wish to acquire the measure of this place."

If this be advice tis pickled to a pinch indeed. I lay motionless in the gloom as the sqweel of an owl momentarily halted the whispers.

"Ye have arrived at the banks of a mighty river whose lustrous surface mirrors the world entire. Thus tis all things eventually come face to face with their reflection. Ye see thy likeness decorate the folds of water. Suddenly tis floated off. Horrified yet helpless ye watch it as tis rendered into the rough torrent where soon no trace remains. Again ye look into the river. There be no more likeness to sweeten thy fancies, only a sombre silhouette eclipsing thy soul. So tis most things go. Yet none the wiser we remain, being unaware of what it was we possessed. Inkblots, knucklebones, vapourish dead, noseless face, hat on head. Red clay clinched, suffocate a mole, dog star lit, farewell thy soul."

## 49

Indifferent to the moon's splendour did the whispered words confine a darkness round my heart that persisted the following day. I had spent the morning skirting a covered runlet braided black with roots that by afternoon opened into a world of radiant glades. Aisles of ancient oaks vaulted a pale sky. Twas not long before I settled into a hollow, riven into the base of one of these giants. A grubby trench indeed, recessed with unclean odours. Nevertheless there was room enough to sit, rest and take stock of my belongings. A meal of dried egg, seeds and blackwine commenced the gradual elevation of my spirits. My weapons were in good order, my coat untarnished. Twas now late afternoon. Through the pallid entrance of my retreat I watched as shadows once again queued onto the world. Father once told me that if all things were what they seemed there'd be little room in this universe for a thought to turn sideways, let alone stand on its head. For certain was uncertainty swarming this realm. Crossing the river had increased an awareness of unease threatening my course. A closer inspection of my hiding place revealed unsettling evidence to compound my trepidation. Twas not a natural feature after all but a gouged chamber, hacked and scratched. Grimy and unkempt with an unkind fragrance twould be reasonable to assume it long abandoned. But reason one feels treads a kinder realm than this.

The nightfall was moonless. Teemed with shrew, rat, moth, weasel, worm and snake. Little for a faery to fear, lest careless beyond account. Even so, were my weapons kept to hand. Snuggled firm within my coat I nestled into a dusty corner affording me full view of the entrance. This be a night put between days to interrupt the fondest life. Fennel, wort and orpin doth brew an avoidance, but not here. So dark a division summons entire perceptions. Else tis the not knowing give thee a nasty turn. As fair and foul doth fly in threes I awaited a final voice from the void to complete the invisible trio. I was not disappointed. For in the early hours, shadows within my shelter curiously multiplied. Even for me within a tree was the world now indistinct. Difficult to locate a single direction. Twas then it spoke.

"Spit in thy spit, if thou spittle at all, thou spittest the quicker for being so small. To spit from up here takes a long time to fall, my spit doth grow cold for being so tall.

"Bleed in thy blood if thou bleedest at all, thou bleedest the sooner for being so small. To bleed from up here takes forever to fall, my blood doth grow old for being so tall.

"See what thou see if thou see at all, see thou the lesser for being so small? To see from up here for being so tall, everything's there, yet nothing at all."

Twas a melancholic chant, sad sounded.

"Topaz yellow as an eye,
Hobs intent for ye to die,
Idols worshipped neath a hill,
Maiden doth her belly fill.
Brocade will thy spirit keep,
Lynage even when thee sleep.
Exclaved now this land doth lie,
Secure thy soul lest it should fly.
Tomorrow's not the time to start,
Afford thy name a cautious chart.

Rejourn. Rejourn. Rejourn."

Then of a sudden did a great moon fulfil the wood entire, curing a portion of dark within the tunnel. The voice resumed, yet quieter for the light.

"Thou hast seen thy name in this message well enough. Once was I a traveller, much like yourself. Come to this land in search of that which had driven me from the realms of love. Graciously greeted by a garden at the river's edge. Unlike thee, however, did I foolishly accept the comfort of its invitations. Thus twas I slept within its borders. There did a foul treachery confiscate the corpus of my dreams. As a consequence I have nothing left. The winds of each season carry what is left of me aimlessly from tree to tree across this wretched land. With each passing year am I transported further and further from the river's edge whence I came, more distant each day from salvation. For were the winds to change, driving me back over the great mirror of the river, might that which has been so despicably taken be revealed once again in the silver of it. Alas, am I not the only one afflicted so. Thousands doth haunt this sphere. Tis best to sleep by day and move by night in this land, if that which ye seek ye wish to find. For tis darkness that unleashes this perfidy. Surely would the natural justice of light expose the measure of its shame. Soon I will be elsewhere. So have a care. Lest that which ye seek, end up there."

## 50

That voice possessed a tremble of my mother's heart. This land be filled with all manner of echoes from that which surrounds it. The morning was bright as faerys' wings, reinforcing my eagerness to be underway. Had the voices not resembled those of my family, their messages might have sounded less significant. As twas, their compulsive combination stalled my quest. An unwelcome delay for sure, but one that I felt in some way might secure my entirety. Reluctantly, I remained within the tree whilst the day did do without. Twas late afternoon when restlessness persuaded me to reacquire the line ascribed by Mr Green, thus pursuing that which I most earnestly desired. Propping my bow against the back wall of the tunnel for safe keeping, I moved to the entrance where by the shadows' dial I hoped to fix a direction. A gradual unfolding of darkness upon the face of the wood murmured the soul. Returning into the shelter, I made my way to the rear and was immediately alarmed at discovering my bow vanished. The where and how of it fit to perplex the keenest eye. I sat in the dark, contemplating the mix of such a mischief. Suddenly, a small doorway opened in the roof of the tunnel directly above me and from it two small heads, mottled as moths, stared down.

"Madam, there be a blockage in our house which hath cruelly curtailed our humble needs—and you are it."

"Yes you are," the other agreed.

"How much longer are you likely to fill our doorway? Mr Slaygrave and Mr Scapeflud hope thy policy be all politeness as we fondly extend our good measure to thy clutter."

"Yes, that we do. By the graces that manage to bear some measure of civility in this wicked world, we do. Do we not, Mr Slaygrave?"

"Fondly sparred, Mr S. Fondly sparred."

Then did the thread of an arm supporting a large three-fingered hand produce my bow.

"Look at this thingywhatsit. It's a fair thought to consider this as evidence that thou hath been dispatched to stumble us. Stumble us indeed. Our legs are not what they were. A thingywhatsit such as this, abandoned without a care on a foreign doorstep, might well have tricked my ancient leg. Not to mention Mr S's."

"A favourable policy Mr S. Favourable indeed. For doth not my leg flare up at a mention. Best written than said. As for you, my little fingybob, thy inclination I'll bet be a percentage toward the in rather than the out. By such a judgement, we invite thee to join thy thingywhatsit for a nibble with the Joineries. An expense we are at liberty to afford now our property hath more of a flow to it."

Eager to repossess my prized bow I accepted without hesitation the convolutions of their invitation. With a brisk jump through the hatch I alighted in the strangest of chambers. A tall cylindrical room, raw wooded, hacked by the same art as fashioned the tunnel. Scattered at random about its gnarled face were an assortment of what I took to be doors. All were cut curiously above our heads. In fact, at floor level there was nothing. By all that makes us different must an eager portion of it have designed my hosts. Their strangeness befitting their property. Truly was their skin mottled as a moth wing vanished on wood. Their tiny heads hairless, their eyes black-beaded as a faery's. Two bow strings for arms but strong hands. The silhouette of their entirety tapered to a dagger's point, being in possession of no more than a single leg apiece. By such a peg were they perfectly balanced in the tall chimney of their home.

"A biped, Mr S."

"Indeed, Mr S."

"Life be far too dangerous to cope with the enthusiasms of two legs. Is it not, Mr S?"

"Indeed, were I to have it, twould be a fixture fit to double thy jeopardy, were one able to choose between the two which be the most favourable."

"Not a choice designed to ease the burden of thy life, Mr S."

"Indeed not, Mr S, indeed not. One leg for one life be my motto. For one leg be more than ample for one day. Two legs be far too reckless. Tis a miracle thy steps are not tied most fearful. Though too much criticism might encourage our guest to think she be something other. I therefore propose imbibition without delay."

"A toast, Mr S. Well called."

And with that he promptly leapt halfway up the chamber wall into one of the distant doorways. An immense jump, ten times his height, that appeared to require no effort at all. A moment later he returned, landed as if by the grace of flight. He held out three goblets and a flask of finest moonglass.

"Tis a drink of unequalled recommendation. Prime tipple. Twill ravish thy heart. Gloss thy eye. Twill ornament thy vernacular, will it not, Mr S?"

"Beyond a doubt, Mr S. Beyond a doubt. Transfigure thy speech till thy tongue be spent of words."

Deftly removing the glass stopper from the flask, Mr Slaygrave cautiously tipped the liquid into our goblets. Twas identical to water by its absence of colour and fragrance.

"A toast, Mr S."

"Indeed, Mr S."

"Here's to the wicked you-know-what. Might its industry capitalise on those whose fortunes are deserving its attention."

"Amen to that, Mr S. Here's to the evil you-know-who. Ne'er the profanity of its uttered name shall gather its designs to our humble estate."

Then was the liquid single swallowed each in turn.

## 51

Now was I more than ever persuaded to the drink's identity. It was water. Courtesy forbade me to express little other than delight. I remained the silent of the three.

"This draught doth flurry the blood. A thousand lives hath flourished in this tree since Blotchliver tunnelled for storage neath the roots of it. Is that not so, Mr S?"

"Tis mightily right, Mr S. Mightily right. For twas there did it permeate the walls of the said basement by enchantment. For no matter how much be taken is it forever replaced. Why alter its intent when tis offered for thy benevolence? Hast thou ever tasted the like, my little unpronounceable?"

I indicated that I had. They appeared surprised.

"A revelation indeed, Mr S."

"Indeed, Mr S."

"May we enquire of the source my slip of a shadow?"

I said of course. For twas as common as knowledge itself.

"Common! Common, you say. Surely not. Were wonders of this gravity common then might evil which so readily stalks this land be but a memory. Is that no so, Mr S?"

"Indeed so, Mr S. Indeed. To see it and taste it is proof enough that were its worth more frequent found, then things which we fear would powerless be."

"Rightly said, Mr S. T'as never been named by us, though we share a history with it. For no name be a justice no name can match. Tis preferable for so honest a gift. For tis inoffensive by sight and smell. Transparent as the fondest souls. So if thy claims are justly founded, name it now."

So I did.

"Water! Water you say! Impossible! Tis black as sin and lives in rivers. Is that not so, Mr S?"

"Justly said. Mr S. Justly said. Water doth infest the common turn, without a doubt. If one were to drink it, then one would imbibe the very souls of the dead. It creates mirrors. It divides worlds. To sum up—it lives in rivers."

I insisted it was not my intention to cause offence and that answers if required should preferably be honest. Tis possible I was mistaken.

"Tis possible thou art sent by trickery to separate us from our prize."

I informed them that no such contrivance had caused our paths to cross, and as a mark of it was I willing to part their company on the instant. They moderated their tone.

"Haste hath toppled many a happy prospect in this world, Mr S."

"Rightly so, Mr S. Let us all be better judged by better judgement."

"Amen to that, Mr S."

Nevertheless, the accusation had tainted their good will and I was increasingly eager to be elsewhere. Besides, the chamber which was lit by threads of wood coated with a mask of grease or oil (one guessed from its odour) was building up a heat difficult to tolerate. If twere ventilated the benefit was negligible. Twas not long before I began to cough. Insisting they show me the door, I was led by a bounce through one of the upper exits into a small oval chamber where the air was less contaminated. Twas cooler too. Less anxious, I perched upon the curve of the wall, as my elongated hosts compelled me to a meal before my departure. They quickly procured a selection of berries and nuts in wooden bowls and placed them on a grey cloth upon the floor. Blackthorn, dogwood, rose, oak and beech also included a quantity of elder and chestnut, for which I have a preference. These were well dried, but perfectly edible, being rich of taste. To wash it down was I once again handed a goblet of remarkable water.

"By all that's honest how can such a drink be what you claim? Tis clear as a scryer's eye. Is that not so, Mr S?"

"Indeed so, Mr S. For is there not at the world's edge a river to lure thee from it, filled with all manner of foulness? See thy reflection. See thy demise. Twill dispatch thee quicker than tooth or claw. Tis common knowledge."

"Common indeed, Mr S. Common indeed. I have heard it this life's length. Tis common as this be rare." He held aloft the flask. "So have a care."

Suddenly, my stomach was gripped by violent cramps, producing a painful spasm wherein I trembled, fitful and breathless. I fell upon the floor. As my hosts left the chamber and closed the door, my eyes widened as I writhed in the dark. Possessed by shivers did I speedily faint away.

## 52

When I awoke, the door to the chamber was slightly ajar. A pale flicker of woodlight from without trembled over the wall, as doth the wing of an orange moth. I was cold. Had the water been a tear-drop more virulent there is no doubt chills would be of little concern. Even so did a painfulness continue to paralyse my movement. I lay in some discomfort upon the grey cloth, my eyes fixed upon the line of danced glimmer signalling a way out. I listened intent for the telltale clump of Mr S and Mr S, whom it was obvious had seen fit to poison me. Yet none approached. Only the customary creaking of oak, sparred by winds without. Twas reassuring to hear its ancient grace creak and whisper. Its clicks and ticks reminding me of home. By degrees fit to test the patience of a heron, were my limbs awakened. Eventually, on all fours, I was able to make my way to the open door. Knelt upon its ledge, I looked down into the funnel of the large chamber. Long curves of shadow now hung twixt the two remaining pinches of flame. I was reminded forceful of the well within the spriggans' hill. Barely visible, the figures of my hosts lay motionless upon the circular floor. If ever an eye contained a blemish, it be this one. Unbuttoning an arrow did I then project it from the bow toward their slumbers, splitting the wood between them. Failing to disrupt their sleep was I fast on its flight. I alighted beside the arrow, where bowlike the arched dreamers lay inert. After easing the blade from the oak, I was prompted to prod Mr Slaygrave with my bow due to the odd contortion of his repose. There was no response. I poked again. The black beads of his eyes were glared yet lifeless. His bump of a belly thrust into the air, though twere a cart crossing the bridge of his body twixt head and foot. With a more forceful nudge did the figure topple complete, though still not awaken. With a hand did I cautiously touch for life. His mottled skin cold as water in a well. It now appeared that my hosts did not poison me after all. For they too had come to grief by the same treachery, though their ability to withstand it was not so ardent. As I stood between the rigid arcs of their corpses, a faint line gradually began to illuminate along the dark floor. A lambency of daylight had reached into the tunnel with the rising sun to filter through the hatch. It too had been left mysteriously ajar. With some haste, I vacated the chamber, fleeing to that which knows best my heart. Tis but worldswork.

## 53

I had not travelled far when I came to a tree fallen across a brook. Twas coated in a jewel of moss yet hollow as a yarthkin's heart. Though damp and dark, twas free and safe. I crawled in. Near the entrance was a good seat of greystone. As I looked out, was I forced by the scope of its door to peer back at recent events, which made me quietly question my resolve to avoid flight at any cost. A judgement I thought as immoveable as Grandmother's words. Thou art free to imagine the dangers so large a world can inflict on one so small. Though twould be opinion fraught with misconception. Specific perils tis true doth advantage take of a negligent mind. Unaided by the art of Elfin tea, doth birds and bats come sample thee. Tis a blend that creates invisibility by illlusion. A transparency which hides us from the want of birds, not bats. For Mr Leatherwing, doth the tea's variability empower our hearing to detect its every move and murmur, be it the distance of thy field. He may chase, but he will find precious little in his own demise. As for the rest, doth a faery's senses unaided 'cept by bow and blade be more than adequate. Besides, without the tea's stimulation to animate the body entire, flight is a burden too great to bear but the shortest distance.

This poison hath disordered my thoughts. I had wandered but the shortest way, yet was exhausted. I needed sleep, lest my shuffled logic mislead me into further menace. Mr Green hath pecked a peril, sure enough. Yet tis a course where no other be found. The voices had spoken well enough, for fair few can trace a memory locked fond in thy soul. Thus tis I have the science of direction and instruction. By the same token could I never abandon my promise to Grandmother. Such undutifulness would be a grave oversight. She was stubborn as oak and long lived by that reputation. A legacy which preserves her daughter to this day. Mother was always suspicious of water, rightly forbidding it past her lips lest boiled or spiced. Tis a pity the Pegs were not party to such counsel. Worried thoughts stalled the afternoon, ferried gently to and fro on watery sounds from under the tree. Eventually, neath a coppery sun, was I lulled into fitful sleep, wherein the mix of these turmoils phantomed a lurid realm.

## 54

Tis true, invisibility doth keep our whereabouts preserved, our domain entire. But tis the magic of our make which protects us from many things in this world, for by it are we rendered untouchable. So when the blunt prod of a shrew's snout tumbled me from my uneven repose, was I left alive to watch the blackball of his body bobble down the damp tunnel. Though was he rebuked by the point of my tongue till vanished. Unspun done, spit sealed quick. Should I be in possession of that stone, which heavy as a mortal soul shone with flawless fire upon my father's table, would even the measure of its saffron eye fail midst so many uncertainties. For now the moon has rolled onto its black road like a silver coin spilt from the eye of a corpse over great groans of oak. Time to be away, lest thy dreams fall foul to such a call.

With soul, silver, shirt and shoes bound safe within my coat's inheritance, plus modest supplies of dried food, weapons and a little wine, was my pace encouraged into the night over fierce weaves of bramble. Tis only the souls of the unknowing that fear the great forests of this world. Nevertheless, I cautioned speed as I crossed a pale avenue of moonlight which overspread the wood in ghostly pools. The giant oaks were gone, revealing the hub of heaven, black as a goblin's heart. Though there be some hope in the faithful diagram of its ancient fragments, yet was there also some unknown breath in all this, keen as elder, foul as bile. I stopped. This place hath embraced too much darkness for its own good. Though fair the floor be framed, yet some mangy menace infest its vicinity. Evil doth sweat with the best of us. This night hath its humour, unbalanced by extremities, best mended with the letting of blood. Tis an infestation unmistakable to any faery long-lived. Yarthkins. Seen best by the invisibility which they keep, and the foul stench of their breath, such is the corruption of their word. Quietly, I hooked an arrow onto the glister of a whisker. Part loaded did I scour the moony wood for any inclination that might betray their poxy carcasses unto my blades. The air was breathless as death. Though they will jeer soon enough, for tis their nature to betray themselves into harm's way, so witless is their want for hurtfulness. Devoid of any goodness, tis said their minds are empty but for fearsome echoes, which rage out of the past beneath their grey eyes. Father said there was a game in all this somewhere. Thus, tis the evil are set free amongst the good, and vice versa, to define that which denies us all. Be that as it may, tis best avoided, lest your life be spilt by their cruelties, merely for thy innards to dot a sentence. Then was the first of their lame chants borne into the air on a putrescence of breath fit to match its artlessness.

"Pluck her wings, burn her coat, pop her eyes, slit her throat."

Pathetic doggerel fouling so noble a night that gloriously indifferent shone about. Yarthkins. How best can I describe them by the genius of thy language? This world be weirdly wrought, twixt the fire and ice of sun and moon wherein most things imagined find form. Thus tis the unimagined form themselves midst the great darknesses that wait about. Twas in one such luckless void the misfortune of their recipe was cast. Take a length of sickly skin, thin as flies' wings. Stretch it carelessly over bones so ugly twould startle a toad. Splodge with all manner of pox and blotches. Riddle twixt these a maze of greasy veins. Soak the aforementioned in a secretion of spittle, nightsoil, phlegm and mucous. Tis now slippier than a fish. What's more, doth it smell worse than one long dead washed ashore in summer's heat. Cut off the stump of its nose, the leaves of its ears, the lids of its eyes. Peel away the lips of its mouth. Far too heartless for hair doth the ugly head now baldly point its six sore holes like pits on a map of sin. Thin arms sprout five long fingers capable of counting any wickedness in this world, delivered on cruel legs, foul-footed. Tis heartless and mindless. Transparent as an empty bottle cast adrift, the message within but a warning to any goodness thus encountered. Yet goodness take heart where the heartless roam. For by it are we fit to conquer by death or life any such encounter.

Now were we run deeper into rootwrithes. Their chants at once close, now distant, suddenly the closer. Their tongues and teeth dark as rotten leaves chattered all about. Even so, for them to catch and me to suffer, must they relinquish invisibility by flight. Thus tis they are opposed to all things. Where we are visible, they are not. Where we burn white are they turned black. And they will need to fly for me to die, for none can match a faery's fleet o'foot. So will they betray themselves, reversing their intent. I shall have them as sure as they are for this game. Now was the chase intensified anew as two were flighted bony black neath moonlight. The juggle of their limbs jerked in ugly leaps about the floor. I waited. Then were they set upon the air, raucous and thin as starved bats, with screels of wings and wounded words clattered. Releasing the poisoned arrow was it faithful run clean through the neck of the first. Its pitiless soul spat blackblood - wrapped twixt the rotten needles of its teeth into woodsweat. With this did rage beset the second to lunge at me direct. A berserk leap that spilt its life upon the length of my dagger, as crazed spasms emptied its lungs of fetid air. Re-arming the bow, was I leapt amongst the youngest trees. Momentarily was the wood re-acquainted with shadows sound. Dark's quiet that resonates with favour souls so tuned. Soon stained a second time as sneers anew filled the air.

"There she be, dangled dainty up a tree. Let's pick her off and cut her throat, suck her gristle, soil her coat."

Thus taunted was the chase renewed. Following a trace of light was I led into a narrow gully, a small waterway that ran between stout roots toward the brook.

Yarthkins were everywhere. The silhouettes of their skeletal capers reeling o'er the wood. The clicking of their clumsy wings wound loud. Once again did I still myself to contemplate the mix of it. Frustrated in their designs, were they the wilder still. Screeding at the bit of their empty ambitions. Given time they will turn upon themselves to satisfy their lusts. Thus tis, one thought doth light their universe. How many blades I must blacken with their blood before this night be ended I cannot tell. With the lurch of their yells grown suddenly distant, I leapt from the trench into a long corridor twixt taller trees. Here was the air floated damp and still. The yarthkins barely audible. Crowds of roots and fallen branches zig-zagged through the gloom. Leaping over honey-coloured fungi, from disc to disc, was the air paved so numerous with their dainty heads, I was afforded a welcome distance from my last encounter. Again I stopped. The stools trembled as gathering clouds snuffed the moon. A night such as this, breathless but for whispered words, could never rock these clever cakes upon which I stand in such a fashion. I remained motionless even to a breath. Suddenly was the moon uncovered. Fresh filled with light was the turbulence plain seen all about. Something was lurking neath the stools. I'll wager ne'er a noose so tightened be as bony or black. Just then was the chant of their intent whispered neath my feet. Then silence. I held my dagger firm. I imagined the entire world hushed as dust. Then, to my horror, were the sails of two enormous black wings scissored into the air before my eyes, striking my hand, casting my dagger into an unlit sea of squirming malice, which now besieged my tiny island. Thus encouraged was my assailant risen misshapen into the night, more hung than hovered, foolishly flicking its head backward, squirting from its grin the hot milky spittle that gargles their crooked necks. Twas in that moment of self-congratulation I took an arrow in hand and poked it through the wall of its blistered belly, thus enabling it to better see how to spell a victory. Then were the shadows of a second and third yarthkin surfaced from beneath the fungus. If I am to live, then I am to fly. So twas without a thought to weigh me down I instinctively leapt into that which guards us evermore. Yet without the tea were all the disadvantages of such an action brought to bear almost immediately. Thus twas within that moment, so desperately acquainted, was I struck unconscious by a branch, or a bird, or a bat, I know not which, and tumbled into the night's unpredictable embrace.

## 56

What cares this ageless world for the insignificant glimmer of a single soul, so briefly lit can scarce be known? Little or less tis best reckoned if ye wish to reckon with it. For by such a calculation will it burn for thee, fierce as any sun in the immensity of all things. Tis worth more than a whistle in the dark by this moon's ghost. What doth he who owns a universe care for a button of such inconsequence were it multiplied as stars? Ye who have listened long have heard precious little to comfort thy lost labour. Yet unanswered doth it not undaunted shine? Doth it not proffer for thee to credit it alone? Long life doth a strong heart require, and by it are we offered no gift greater. What be good for nothing shall nothing find. Such an end as this hath crossed my mind when uncertainties lashed and galed my home though twere all at sea. Barely am I able to recognise what destiny there now be to illuminate this nightstark.

My fall hath broken more thoughts than bones. Though am I much hurt when moved. I have a split wing, torn coat and no dagger. More disturbingly hath the tumble scattered not just my wits but my arrows too. Yarthkins are persistent hunters. They will sniff this misfortune soon enough. Theirs is a nose for trouble. Listen! Their cries approach relentless as the greatest of certainties. The black filled with squeals fit to shiver any resolve. Unable to run, unable to fly, I frantically pick at leaves for my lost blades. The disorder of the yarthkins approach, plainly heard by a frenzied ruffle of cruel wings. Where are those arrows? Too late! For now was the dark twice darkened by a circle of silhouettes, danced joyously at finding that which they so desired hurt, hurt the more. So many years have I lived alone that death requires no introduction. My soul so small as to show our greatest loss unnoticed go. However, yarthkins have a reputation for cruelty unmatched by any, except men. Though by luck can their murderous desires sometimes outweigh their relish for torture. Were I fit by reason to think it, fortune hath abandoned this quest. Then was I unceremoniously pinned to the ground by a weight of black wings for their butchery to commence. I saw the trees. I saw the stars. I saw the dark. Then nothing.

## 57

"Where hast thou but by luck abandoned ended? Sound judgement for a promise broken? Remember thy mother's mother? How is it thy life hath failed by such means?"

Grandmother?

"Tis I, my little spriggit. Or is it the hobthrush, toothless and fluteless come to glower? For this domain doth embody in countless manner many an evil thought. All that hath gone astray, and more besides, doth live in this land I fear. Were it boiled or buried or pricked with a lancet. Thy soul hath found its egg well enough."

"Thimblestar."

Mother?

"During falling sickness hath I seen thee, when the moon doth wax and feathers boil. Thou art genuine enough, though too far too to see, being vapourish as that which hath caused thee great harm. Thou hast ignored warnings to thy peril. There be too much water in all this for fair or favour. Beware. Thou art no better seen by me than by the eye of an apple."

"Sister."

Winkleprimbell?

"I have a small table fashioned of hazel. Tis pretty with three legs. Upon it sits a jar of darkness, wherein a thought doth live as any creature. Of late were many seen within its eye that bore thee malice. Swam like teeth in the dark syrup of its void. Thus twas with ease were they borne away. Thou hast been careless beyond account. Thy soul jeopardised by unequal turns of events. Therefore should ye know that they who would otherwise suffer are made beyond it by thy recklessness."

"Listen!"

Father?

"Thy make hath salted thy soul well enough. There be little need in all this to raise a horse or balance a head on a rod of hazel. I have spoken to thee before concerning deceptions. Wherever the night is ye have little need of it. Deceive the sorrow of the morrow. Simply open thy eyes."

## 58

So I did. It was morning. My demise had been but a dream. Yet thought up so darkly as to shame the cruellest night. Made worse than if twere real by the memory of it. Though was I greatly pleased to raise myself unharmed from the sapped grey leaves into the lit wood. Relieved that the ordeal had left me entirely unhurt, my coat untorn, my belongings intact. I determined then by haste to place as much distance as my strength would allow between this place and my next sojourn. As I ran, the mix of previous events raced giddy in my mind's eye. There was no doubt I had in truth encountered yarthkins. That now there were three where all should be. Did I not have the stains of black blood upon my coat and hands to prove it? My dagger was missing, an arrow too. And there was no question concerning the blow that rendered me insensible. The left side of my head, neck and upper back sore to the touch. By reason of the here and now was the rest consigned to dreams by the merciful collision that must have fired me from the reach of my pursuers. But what of the voices? Grandmother, Mother, my Sister, Father. Were they real, or imagined too? This wood be worked by words. The entirety pollinated by whispers both wondrous and wicked. Had not Grandmother warned me so? Or was it once again the bounty of this place boasting its path? One thing however was indisputable. Yarthkins never travel by day. Tis not that they fear it, for they fear nothing. Tis simply they are rendered incapable by it. Why this is I know not. How tis the light hath stolen so much fortune, thus confirming the dark so luckless here, be another mystery. Were the world entire so discoloured twould be owned by men alone. Never was a course so ill-favoured. Though now the wood began to open out. Oakfern faced to lure such lights as ladder a heaven. Tis lordly here. An ancestry never more nobly attended. Guardians of giant elm, beech and oak form a common splendour. Driven but watchful was I hurried twixt its lovely ways. By late afternoon I began looking for a secure place in which to spend the night. Reasonably confident I had outrun the unspeakable, I waded watchful through luminous pools of lightfall. Where in such grandeur might a soul to shelter take? Where so well-formed might the wary escape persecution? Father was right. There be a game in all this somewhere. Tis but worldswork.

## 59

Neath a peeling flap of dead bark, high set and unseen, was I fortunate to discover a dainty nest long vacated. Twas a merit to its art. Spent of energy, I fell into its feathery pocket, oblivious to an approaching night of mischievous storms. I was awoken by thunders to a black event indeed. Rain and wind set upon the world as though keen to destroy it. My tree rocked in its spell though twere wandwaving. Yet this little ship wove of nothing more than twigs, feathers and mosses hath found a perfect harbour. By so simple a science was it more than a match for so great a commotion. Light and dark in turns glared over the wood in blinding flashes. Thou hast witnessed such things during darkest times. Then did a mighty spark pierce the night, flared into the heart of my domain, its lurid fire illuminating my face—and that of the creature sitting opposite. How the figure appeared so suddenly I know not. Twas as though the lightning itself had deposited it. Twas sat squat square in its batskin coat, though twere a leathery toad, its reckless head a folded dollop of troubled skin plonked upon broad shoulders, though twere a crow's dropping on a stone. This was two-thirds hid neath a parched mask fashioned from a bat's head, the distorted gums of which concealed the creature's eyes. Its mouth too was toadlike. Long, thin, lipless, toothless. Twas as though someone had placed a rule from ear to ear and drawn a thin line twixt misery and joy. Never was a mouth more redundant. For ne'er a snack popped in or a sound popped out. Unwelcome as it was, I had not the will to evict it. Occasionally twould raise its short thick arms as though to wave, both hands being unmatched well beyond the left and right. For not only did they differ in proportion considerably, but the smaller, the right, made up for what it lacked in size by owning seven fingers, four more than its bigger twin. Its legs were toadish too, preferring to exit the ball of its body from the sides rather than the base. Thus twas they folded without a care into the shadows of its coat. Yet this was no toad, its woven belt supporting a hook of bone, a fine waspsting dagger, a mirror, leather beaker and grey pouch tied with root that stank considerably. Thus was, we sailed such a night, eye to eye in silence. My hands firm fastened on the weapons neath my coat.

By day break the storms were passed. Twas impossible to tell if my guest slept or no, so narrow was the withered mouth of the mask through which it viewed the world, its hem of black gums lined with a twisted row of white needles. There was something else too, criss-crossing the sore grey skin of its rippled neck. Scars. Lots of scars. The hands were stained yellow, its black nails grown and curved from the crooked fingers it had plunged into the woollen lining of the nest. Its legs and feet were bare. Worn out, if looks were to judge. A mangled lining of toes and nails atop each festered pad. But the coat was exquisite. The tools fine crafted. The belt buckled silver. It took the rattle of a magpie to eventually stir it into the new day. Instantly, it lurched up the nest wall, perching on its brim. Revolving the pudding of its head to scour the world revealed a circular hole in the back of its mask that again uncovered more of the cruel scars. With the twitch of a wave it signalled for me to follow. It scurried down the bark with rat skill, pouncing onto the floor of the wood, landing square set, hands gripped to belt, legs akimbo, though it owned the world. Then did it swagger away, its thick legs slapping each footfall into the leaves. Once again it beckoned me to accompany. Once again I complied. Preferring for the present to be led by that which I would not wish behind me.

For one beset by doubts, Mr Pipitop's confident yet ungainly walk had such a reassurance of stride that twas easy to secure thy hopes to it without too much question. More a dance than a step, his body was bounced and bumped on the stocky springs of his jouncing legs. Thus twas we were propelled into a quarter of the world where the sky fell behind the trees in sorrows of grey. A great flux of rootweave disrupted the floor neath the slap of his rotten feet. Here was the fix of it a statue to its past. Ancient in the air. The leap of its world run through with foretime. An old wood indeed. A universe anchored deep in earth.

We had been walking for some time before Mr Pipitop stopped abruptly, balancing the block of his body on a black stone. His right arm jerked a crooked finger into the air. Thus indicated, was my gaze set upon the oddest display. A gallery of corpses no less. Birds, squirrels, mice, rats, moles, weasels, voles, bats, but most disturbingly—a yarthkin. Twas unmistakable. Its torn carcass hung like a black sail in the still air. All were weather-worked well beyond the measure of their lives. Their ragged bodies dangled from lengths of crude cord. Mr Pipitop spat viciously onto the stone. Twas the first time I had seen his mouth move. He then slapped his left foot squarely onto the ball of yellow phlegm before resuming his swagger into the darkening wood.

As our way became increasingly sombre and unpredictable so too did my guide. He began to cough and mumble. He would stop to violently shake his shoulders or jerk a limb. The more I followed the more I looked. The more I looked the more convinced I became of a torment afflicting his spirit. Twas by this scrutiny I fashioned him as a kind of puppet figure, his body pulled, twitched, and steered in turns about the shadows of the wood. Twas as if when his body moved his mind was caught out. Yet were his legs so stout that no such disturbance above was ever allowed to unbalance so assured a gait. He seemed not to tire or alter his step. If I stopped, he would do likewise, without ever turning to look for such a cause. Yet his ears (if indeed he owned any) were concealed within Mr Leatherwing's head, his mask. If the condition of his feet and hands were any measure, it was reasonable to assume his hearing was not the detector of my whereabouts, twas something other. At each turn he would cough up phlegm and stamp it underfoot. A slippery trail for sure, spat with purpose.

Now were the roots of this great entanglement wove tighter still. Twas a world squeezed into steely knots of green wood. Slippery, unlit. Mr Pipitop became more agitated by the turn, scratching his scars strenuously, causing tiny beads of black blood to weep from his wounds. He pulled at his clothes, gripped his mask, then inspected the items hanging from his belt as though he had not seen them before. Twas well into the day when we reached a large white stone wedged twixt roots, tight as an eye in its socket. Mr Pipitop took to it as any who likes a stage. I watched as he sniffed the air with all the gravity of ritual. Swaying to and fro as though to beckon any speck of favour. Predictably twas spat and trod underfoot. He bowed about, mumbling, scratching. Leaping from the stone he took off down a dark gully lined with wet pebbles, his pace no longer ponderous. Twas a vigorous jaunt twixt tangled banks. He urged me follow with the tilt of his head. Thus twas the tilt of mine by abeyance inclined toward increasing unease at vulnerability thus persuaded.

## 61

At the end of the gully the pebbles faded into a sandy bank, which in turn lifted us out of the damp onto a dry plot of land. Twas a long narrow promontory risen from a bed of saturated leaves. Mr Pipitop ambled to its crest with no loss of pace. The causeway itself was grassed dainty. Each blade small and fine as an elf's sword. Yet was the whole pale of it overhung with unnatural quiet. The air floated in a stale gloom, surrounded fast by scratches and scribbles of thorny wood. Mr Pipitop stopped. Beckoning me to his side was I introduced to a narrow track that ran along the summit to the far end of the ridge. Twas just the thread of a way, but visible nonetheless. Mr Pipitop now applied a caution to his step, so deft as to steer the lump of his body precisely along the path so ne'er a blade of grass was trod. He progressed with some caution, before bowing his masked head into the stilled air. Signalling a halt did he then survey this gloomy prospect from the vantage of the mound. Halfway along the causeway, we were now able to see the end of it more clearly. At its furthest point, a slip of wood smoke appeared to rise up from out of the earth behind a roundish grey stone. Beyond that, the path descended out of view, no doubt back into the waterlogged world from which we had risen. As we approached the smoke, Mr Pipitop began wiping his hands upon his coat in a distracted state. The oddity of his behaviour no doubt compounded by the disorder of this entire domain. I too had become sceptical as to the wisdom of this day's work. Never was I more lost in a world I call my own. Twas a grim reminder of the predicament I had come to know. Approaching the stone twas clear to see it rounded smooth, two-thirds buried in the summit's red soil. Lying next to it was a large wooden club. The smoke appeared to rise from a small fissure just beyond the sunk stone. Mr Pipitop stooped to retrieve the club. Paying no heed to me whatsoever, he swung it with some force onto the rounded stone. The blow produced a thud, dull as the day in which we stood. Immediately, the stone began to move. Mr Pipitop dropped the club into the grass. Then was the stone wobbled aslight before rising up out of the earth to reveal itself as an almost perfect grey sphere. A black rod speedily propped it from below against the lip of the hole in which it previously sat. Without further ado, Mr Pipitop lowered himself unceremoniously through the hole into the ground. Once again, I was beckoned to follow by a vanishing wave. Tis easy to reckon that which conceals a Pipitop could hide a trick or two. This hath a seclusion beyond the wish of most. Tis so hushed even good sense be unheard. There be some dishonesty here that goodness cannot fail to find. As a precaution, I loaded my bow for the measure of it. Approaching the hollow, a lambency of welcome light crept out into the gathering dark of the cold wood. Twas a welcome sign. Yet did I remain ill at ease. Looking through the hole, I was encouraged to gaze down into a white cavern, well lit, bright and clean. A sturdy ladder counted the way in. Tis difficult to say why I stepped onto the rungs that lowered me out of the night into that sunken dwelling. Did not my heart whisper it ill-considered? As I descended, the bar was hastily removed, allowing the great ball to fall back, sealing the entrance above my head with a thump to wake thy senses, be they ever so late. Thus tis, our follies confine us to our fate.

## 62

Tis foolhardy to think evil be consigned to the dark places of this world. For half an eye will reveal the light balanced with equal measure. So it was in that brightest of places I came face to face with the darkest of creatures. How was it Mr Pipitop had led me with ease to this secluded rendezvous? Perhaps his indifference to my will drew me the closer. It mattered little. For the full measure of my imprudence had buried me with that which at all cost we endeavour to avoid — a goblin. In truth we have no name for such a creature, for no name will fit it. Yet Goblin sits upon this story well enough, equal-fitted to the conjure of thy words. Its skin white as the chamber in which we stood, its hair grey as the ash which it ate. Thin black lips, suspended from warted ear to warted ear, peeled apart a line of thick spittle, uncovering a mouth so crammed with teeth twas like an open bag filled with shards of flint. Eyes white as owl's eggs concealing the blackest thoughts. Clothes plain stitched, yet elegant nonetheless. Gowned red from neck to ankles, white-collared, white-belted. Sleeves rolled up to rest upon the shelves of its crusty elbows, exposing the customary red tattoos, which they pierce into their tough skin with barbs of hawthorn dipped in the blood of their victims. Thus tis they are riddled with these designs coloured by another's sorrow. At the ends of these braided trunks hung two six-fingered hands. Decorating its neck, silver set, was what I took to be a human tooth. Tucked into its belt, a small mirror and a rare snake's-tooth dagger. How better to earn from such disadvantage than by patience? Thus twas by forethought I lay my weapons up and sat where instructed. Twas an unfriendly voice that eventually filtered through the storm of teeth.

"Welcome. I trust Mr Spiffle 'ere was behaved enough. For him to turn up with something pretty as yourself, he must have performed his duties well salted." He grinned, consuming half his face with teeth. "I shalln't be denied by a pig's jaw or shoes on fire. Never an apple shall I eat lest me body with wind be stitched. Tis by the belt of me face am I cast. Me mother was ugly as a human baby fresh borned. Though her skin thrust a froth some three hundred year or more. Me father stank of ragwort. Could cover a cat with water. Stole silver from the eyes of human corpses. See this 'ere?" He pointed to the tooth hung about his neck. "A king's tooth, that is. Rare as Spiffle's mercy. Father was boiled alive by misadventure. Could talk a bee to death afore poppin' its eyes. Mr Spiffle 'ere, tis best to see him as a silhouette or masked as tis ye met, for no amount of lead could flatter the pox of his face. See 'ow 'e hides." Mr Pipitop had retreated to the darkest corner afforded. "Would take more than mouseskin to charm so evil an eye. Be warned. Spiffle be as likely not to kill thee should ye flitter out of step as I be seen cavorting with an elf. Ain't that so, Mr Spiffle?"

Mr Pipitop cowered at the creature's every move. Thus twas the entirety of his wounds were explained. For such a master as his be never served by love or devotion. Such credits are hard won, less easy lost. Goblins eat worms. They suck blood from the noses of their victims. They eat their own kind. By such consummations they imagine their knowledge and strength is inherited. They're addicted to asterion. Drink blackroot beer. Thus tis their humour with the world be long gone.

## 63

Tis not uncommon to find goblins housed in the skulls of the dead. You would be amazed at the proximity of these creatures to all men. Yet by their ingenuity are they never uncovered. They are given names at birth that by oaths sworn are kept secret. Father once claimed a dubious acquaintance with one he nicknamed Wudgut. So shall I call this one. They tolerate little—even offers refused. As a consequence, two goblets of blackbeer were served to embellish the anticipated presentation of its home.

"Men and goblins be ever so close. Thus tis we lay claim to their heads. Tis common knowledge. This 'ere pan of bone was shot through with that there ball o' lead. It came through on this side." He pointed to the floor. "Shattering the bone, see. Then his pathetic grip on the world flew out of the aforementioned 'ole allowing us to fly in. Stroke o' luck I calls it, finding it all tucked up 'ere by the encouragement of its own door. The rest of 'im makes a merry maze for 'iding things."

So twas the geography of this domain was explained. The raised causeway along which we had walked was a burial. The corpse of a man, shot through the skull with a ball of lead. Interred on his side in a shallow grave had the years unattached him from all that he was. His forgotten bones scratched and gnawed by all manner of things inclined to that service. Easy sniffed by any goblin, Wudgut and his assistant soon had the skull emptied and cleaned. Their hard work rewarded with the discovery that the damage to the bone lay underfoot and the cause for this (the lead ball) was still in situ, creating a perfect stopper for the doorway they had cut gaining access.

Twas ingenious. Well lit and clean. So clean I was led to comment on it. This was met by a retort spit through teeth though each word be boiled.

"Dirty work be best seen by it."

Thus tis the lives of such creatures are reasoned.

## 64

Then was a fire risen in a copper bowl. A bluish light passed about. Tis said that goblins extract marrow from the bones of buried children. That they work it into a grease containing wolfbane, parsley, hemlock, soot and fat. Rolled into strips is it baked black, then salted. Chewed for a thought does it dye the gravel of their teeth. That they suck the eyes of frogs. Eat the livers of their victims raw. Sip bitter fluids ground from pine for perpetuity. Wudgut's larder was well -stocked. Blood of lapwing, molefat, aconite, poplar leaves, sweetflag, toads' feet, slugloaf, snailcake, mothsalt, specklespin, owlfroth, to name but a few.

"I likes me food unprepared. Least ways most things I eat ain't prepared for the eventuality." He smiled the entire service of his teeth to spit the dot. "Tis rare for the likes of thee to be seen with the likes o' me. Never waste what's given searchin' for that which ain't. For never was a world more cautious of surprises. Yet there be food for thought in every day's passin'. The fetish of thy coat interests me. How is it you ain't unseen in the up above? Thou hast trod a dangerous path. Perhaps too dangerous. Me father was born in a horse's skull. Dined on flaxseed to spite the wisdom of them that thinks they know it all. Were me heart a ball o' rags stuffed with grain, or me head less set than a well of 'em, no better could I have judged the day to day of this life. Were me organs replaced with stones dined on snakeweed, I fancy me wisdom could match that of a man's. Look about. See how easy it is to replace their minds with something more useful. Such as a stool, or an oven. I sits in 'ere and boils me food. I stitch me clothes. I keens me tools. Tis them without that fashions me reputation. Too many thoughts applied thoughtless be the science of their augury. Truth is, I have a soul more bitten by their devil than any benefit fit for 'em. They have come to believe that all that is good be somewhere they ain't. Were they told to soak their wings in honey so's to sweeten their flight they'd 'ave an inclination for it. 'Ere, try a cup o' fingertea."

Iron pans spat upon the stone of the oven. Iron rods stirred the grume. On a diet boiled beyond the use of most, they procure great physical strength. Twould be easy for two of them to fell a human child had they a mind to do so. Yet even the obscurities of their reason secures our realm by total avoidance with thine, lest the latter by voices now almost unheard requires a union.

## 65

Now was the air within the skull transformed into a heated miasma by the ritual of Wudgut's kitchen. Selecting an iron rod would he first inspect the symbols forged along its length by running a fingernail over them, before plunging the red hot bar into the pot, both heating and stirring the food in turn. Twas a procedure as likely to cook me as twas the crop. Sensing my predicament was Mr Spiffle by the click of a summons ordered to re-open the door. As he scrambled to his duties, his master continued to talk.

"That's right Mr Spiffle, open the 'ole. We don't want our guest suffocated before she has savoured the delights of me kitchen. That wouldn't do at all. Besides, I ain't boiling such a fix for the ignorance of your palate. I think it proper that you remove your coat."

A large white hand was extended toward me whilst the other gripped a bar of hot iron.

"Best be comfy. Preserves the occasion. Besides, I'd be cut to the quick if you left us before the full weight of me hospitality could be bought to bear."

Wudgut was wise to the fact that I would never attempt an escape without my coat. He knew that if the chimney-door was propped wide enough, it would not be impossible for me to clear it with a single leap. Reluctantly, I unbuttoned the front, then untied the inner tethers of my most valued possession. Once removed would I be fully disposed to the mercy of the merciless. Taking the coat did he then hold it up for inspection, turning it this way and that over the flame of the oven.

"It's a lovely thing. Light too. Light as air. Even so, my concern for your comfort compels me to confiscate it the while, lest you be tempted from us."

He placed it into one of the natural cavities that probed the dwelling all about.

"Like all good hosts, I be riddled with a tale or two. One of me uncles followed a mole down a hole. A common practice with us. After a short crawl, and not a lot o' digging, he bumped into a body in a box. A human burial. I mean, how considerate can you be without realising you're considerate at all? They're big, they're simple to find, everything inside is usually easier to use. There's quite often bits of cloth for importancies, brass you can melt for tools, wood. Loads o' space, in an' out of the body. Downright thoughtful, I calls it. What's more, the mole who led to such fortune retraces his steps and bumps into me uncle who promptly kills him. Molefat, very useful. Molefeet, excellent cutting tools. Molefur, the best of bedding. Were luck a thing to count, me uncle'd be pressed for numbers. See how easy it is to start a day with nothing, yet end it with all that entitles a smile. Never be too fussy, lest misery be thy design, that's what me father use to say. I eat spiders. Why do I eat spiders? Because they're plentiful. They're all over the place. I plucks off the legs and eats the bodies. Spiffle eats the legs. He'd eat yer droppings were they wrapped in brown cloth. Ain't that right, Spiffle?"

Mr Spiffle had returned to his corner, where I think he crouched in the vain hope of living unnoticed.

"A goblin hasn't a friend in the world. Not a one. That's why we never starve. 'Cause we eat our enemies."

He chuckled as he poured the steaming food out of the pan into two large dishes. It looked as appetising as wet cement.

"Good cooking relies on secrecy. I never let a guest know what's in store for 'em."

There was no question that Mr Wudgut was proud of his domain. I never imagined such a creature to be so fastidious or organised. But my apprehensions concerning the food remained. Looking boiled beyond hope, I was more than a little surprised to find it contained tastes best described as intense. Though of what I had no idea. Wudgut's wormy lips peeled apart a smile wide enough to conceal many things, though ne'er a truth need fear, for plain seen in the whiteness of those eyes was the blackness of his soul.

## 66

Goblins are sleepless creatures. Father had told me of this. In a realm of stolen dreams they would have little to fear. Unlike thy mind, which is as the earth upon which ye stand, half light, half dark, wherein sleep procures their union. So twas in the mind of this man we sat together separated by the gurgle of the pot. Questionable hospitality prompted the story of my journey to be told. Wudgut was intrigued. Picking up what I took to be a wooden plate, he promptly snapped it in two before dipping a portion into the food. Twas in fact a large biscuit that shed its gritty crumbs in a black hail over the table. A hard and colourless diet requiring more strength to eat than it offered. When both food and story were spent, Wudgut signalled Mr Spiffle to repair the table. Obediently he swept the crumbs into this bowl, before creeping back to the pale assurance of his favoured shadow, the swagger of his former walk reduced by cruel subservience to little more than a grovel.

"Mr Spiffle 'ere needs little to fuel the agitations of his nature. Yet will he endure all this in preference to suffering change. So immovable is the torment of his life. So strong his mistrust of the unknown. He 'ates change. Were goodness itself dispatched to offer 'im the fondest alternative he would snuff it out. Thus tis those without a care can rule the careless. He will scorn any fortune offered. Be warned, lest any bribe proffered afford his displeasure."

What make of creature this poor servant was remained a mystery. His appearance contradicted his diet, for he ate virtually nothing. Wudgut's questionable patronage had presumably provided his meagre belongings. He was not a goblin by any cast, though twas rumoured one may serve another in such a fashion to settle a debt. For Spiffle too could sleep to slip the shackles. A realm where in all the years of the world a goblin has never trod. Though doubtless never a one lost a wink with regret.

## 67

To the left of Wudgut's shoulder was the night revealed black and chilled as a gem. An iron rod inscribed with the letters IDAMAGAN was plunged into the oven's base, arousing the embers. Midst a commotion of jumpy light, Wudgut emptied a pan of ashes onto a crimson glass plate. Whilst adding water was it stirred to a paste. Finally twas cooled by the waving of a large insect wing, wielded in both hands, almost mesmeric over the mix.

"Were it not a tendency to eat most of me guests, I'd be famed for me ashes. Next to frog's eyes sucked neath moonlight there be nothing finer. By me fateless heart I swear it so. Tis as sure as me mother born in a goat's skull or a stone cast to thunder. Or that men be evicted beyond measure of reason. They have mispronounced me well enough. Do we not know the workings of this world wherein they claim their wisdom? They assume much. Fortunes great have they consigned to the graves of their dead. Tis arrogance that fills the earth with the clatter of their buried treasures. Yet was it not this clatter that awoke the first of us by chance into this world? Spinning in the stars was it fated thus to chime the loss of men to our gain. So it goes that neither anger nor jealousy ever stained our hearts. The best thought a man ever had be that of a goblin's."

With the air moderated, Wudgut ordered the chamber resealed. The clay oven began to cool. Spiffle curled into a shadow at the base of what appeared to be the severed foot of a hare draped with samite. From the centre of the shattered floor, the wooden ladder counted nine broad rungs to the stopped hole above. The prop that manoeuvred the lead ball was plainly man-made, possibly an enormous brooch pin, its tapered length and plait still visible neath the blight of years. Around these, cluttered a circle of fixtures salvaged from the dead of men. Coins for a table, brass for stools, wood for shelves and panelling. Six tapers cut or puddled natural in the bone lit the scene. What air doth know, smoke will show. So twas with interest I watched their sooty threads exit neath a curtain of shabby silk concealing a proximity near the mouth of the skull. Wudgut reposed himself upon the length of the hare's hind foot, covering his legs with the samite, propping up his toothy head with the angle of an arm. Twas impossible to judge where those lidless eyes were looking. For in the deception of their vacant stare were ye left to imagine the worst. Between the oven and the curtain a store of simorat with lengths of twisted hawthorn were gathered, behind a flat stone covered with grey cloth. This was to be my bed. Though in truth would there be little comfort to be had by it. For were it spat by the toad could it falter to mark a grave.

## 68

"As any sword worth its weight doth bleed, or a giddyboard pose the question, or golden bowl comfort a soul dangerously travelled, tis fair to bet the likes of us be rarely met. Have not the shifty shapes of night delivered many an encounter. Yet none so rare a trance as thee. By the ointments of me skin or the pattern of me nails tis so."

Leaning forward from his repose Wudgut tapped the bony floor twice with a black fingernail. Spiffle was immediately roused to snuff out four of the tapers. By this smallest of summons were my apprehensions greatly increased. For now was the chamber bloomed dark.

"Me mother was borned with one eye. A suspicious one at that. Through it the world was a question she had no answer for, scrutinising every measure of every day double-time. Nothing was concealed from that eye, yet all things were hid. Twas a paradox me father pondered on his stone chair. Eventually he killed and ate her. I chewed on one of her legs for days. She had skin tough as newborne bone. Sour as specklespin. By the Odal O'Gandogap, ne'er waste what's given. Thus tis the dead find life, the living consume their dues."

Wudgut's conversation was as overcooked as his food, yet no less intense. In the darkness of that man's skull were the thoughts of my host cleverly concealed by his mix of words. Thus twas an intent began to gather its ominous form in that oval gloom.

"The world without grows ever fearful of its own shadow. The river that sees all things grows ever deeper, flows ever faster. So the feeble-minded would have us believe. According to their misguidance tis a realm divided into good and evil, where in fact tis simply the edible and inedible. They would see mystery in a fart and count it significant."

For a while we sat in silence. The oven continued to cool. Its flutter of faint ticks and taps pattered all about. Now and then, the tapers whispered hiss.

"A goblin doth repose yet never sleep. Sleep is a plague that hinders the worthless. Take Spiffle 'ere. Half his life wasted the more lubricating the redundancy of it. Deliberating over the crumbs of his labours. The gods of men hath consigned them to a fool's errand. Tis small wonder they spend half of what little they have forgetting the other half. I fancy a bite o' wormgum and blackbeer."

Once again Spiffle was compelled from his hide by the mere nod of Wudgut's head.

"As sure twas me father ate me mother's significant eye doth good and evil taste identical."

His bidding attended, Spiffle erased himself as best he could in the loop of a shadow.

"Never was a man's head better set than by the clutter of a little death. Tis comforting to think we be hid by such thoughtlessness. Life be deathfed, my little flitterfit, deathfed."

## 69

Flitterfit! It seems now that a thousand years of days hath passed since the temperament of my sister's flight persuaded me to give her that very name. Flitterfit. A nick-nack-name, secret as any sworn in goblins' oaths. A name that has lit the bloomdoom of this wretched night as if twere fifty tapers. Yet how Wudgut had come to utter it unknowing its make is a mystery, yet one within which he hath unwittingly sparked a glimmer of hope. Thus twas the sharp edges, with which we kiss the unwelcome, were set a-shining. I was reminded too that where there be a name there be an owner. This journey hath clouded my view of a previous world. A world familiar as those who had spoken into it. Perhaps the whisperers of this realm are after all no less doubtful than their names. If the hand of my sister had reached this far, it was reasonable to assume that those of my entire family may have followed suit.

The night was slow to pass. Spiffle was fidgety as summer lightning. Wudgut motionless as dead air. Yet was the entirety of it now chimed along by the ringing of my sister's second name. Flitterfit. Quiet as a taper's hiss did I whisper the grip of it. Each letter gathered on the tongue hot as snuffspit. Flitterfit. Then in the shift of a second the remaining tapers failed. Shadows were born into shadows anew. Here was the whispered commerce of dreams and dark set free, for ne'er a thing be seen to hinder their cause. Here could a breath of air tumble our entirety into the stars, so hushed were the reaches of this buried chamber. Suddenly Wudgut sat bolt upright. Swivelling himself briskly round was he the next moment standing motionless before me, his head tilted to one side. Were I to survive an attack, it would be necessary for me to retrieve my coat before attempting an escape behind the curtain, where only a questionable exit beckoned. Much to my relief, however, Wudgut remained motionless. Spiffle made to move but was instantly froze by a vicious order spat through a saw of teeth. We were instructed not to move but listen. Sure enough, a trace of shuffled words distantly circled our chamber. Muted, then faded, then set to murmur upon the ball of the door. We listened. So twas a confirmation of the hope prompted by my sister's name was affirmed through the familiarity of those faint voices. Though how and why that should be so remained unclear.

## 70

"This be it, Mr S. The home of the evil-you-know-who. Never was a place easier to find by merit of our desire to avoid it."

"More honest words be rarely aired in so dishonest a place. But thou hath a way with not just the word but the way itself, Mr S. For by the bones of a bare penny, thou hast indeed navigated our agilities to the door of the wicked-you-know-what, by such haste that its dishonesty was no more thought of than was twas reached."

"Have a care, Mr S. This place hath no regard for the common tongue. Words that contain a truth be fit to choke us, rather than merit our wit. Have we not before now witnessed good intent no sooner borne from our lips as evaporated in this unfriendly disposition?"

"Indeed we have, Mr S. Indeed we have. Never was an invite more disgracefully betrayed. Tis no wonder all good be so breathless in such a place."

"Thou hath shamed the same by shrewdness, Mr S. Shamed it."

"Tis a duty that the rank of our make hath bestowed on precious few, Mr S. Precious few. Credentials I hasten by increased impatience for an honest outcome to this night's work, did we not with consciences clear as that which hath no name, but seeing fit to deal us both to death, do I now unhesitatingly call traitor, apply our office as spies to the evil-you-know-who in a faith that binds such matters."

"Well said, Mr S. Well said. Thou hath added the mix of this deceit to which the sum of it hath by some trickery eluded us. Let us hope that he who, by torments of threat pressed so pure an eye to common spy, though was that questionable duty, performed with ne'er a jot of malice to the comings and goings of those unfortunates, who by the hanker of so malevolent a will, took cruel advantage of our benevolence to betray their whereabouts, let us hope the tail doth now own a head to speak the truth."

"Pickled to a pinch, Mr S. Pickled to a pinch. For has he not by endless questioning claimed knowledge of all things? If the answer be hid, surely twill hide in such a place as this. Death be a questionable realm, Mr S. Questionable indeed. I never heard a thing that lived speak favourable of it. Oft have I wondered how, having turned lifeless, they fared in so relentless a place. I fail to find anything of comfort in the prospect of it."

"Never were the witless so exposed by the facet of a thought, Mr S. This entire fabric hath confused and compelled us into a luckless night not of our desiring. I fear the office of spy hath betrayed good will and cast us twixt night and day eternal. A realm starved of any prospect, by my reckoning, lest the evil-you-know-who be pressed to assistance."

"Since returning home to find our bodies dead as sparks fallen on water, whereby no access can be gained to that luckless quarter evermore, hath this night, I fear, reaped the profit of our trade."

"A reasonable assumption, Mr S. Reasonable indeed. I fear we may have betrayed those abilities enabling us to elevate a presence beyond our sleeping bodies to roam the wider world at will. A bounty dear and gentle as that which we were gifted neath our tree, yet saw fit to condemn us. Tis time to reckon with it, Mr S, and there need be little trepidation attached when all is considered."

"After you, Mr S."

"After you, Mr S."

"As neither hath the greater need, let politeness collude the politic into a union as befits the joineries."

## 71

Not a moment later, the Pegs were hovered before us within the chamber. By the colour of their skin did they appear less dead than when last we met, though twas obvious that what floated before us was alive beyond reasonable threat of losing it.

Wudgut's voice remained passive, yet pitched as if to pry a second demise from the intruders fumbled before him. Supporting his anger by reclining onto the hare's foot, he spoke in stony tones. "Well well well. This night hath spit and pissed all at once. If it isn't Dung and Snivel, legless as worms, wriggled hence to trespass their insignificances onto the undeserving. Thy bodies, gentlemen, be as impaired as thy manners. Were it not for an obvious lack of substance in this matter, rest assured thy stricken souls would stock me larder for this unwarranted intrusion."

Not surprisingly, the Pegs made no reply to these insults, appearing momentarily to fade in our midst.

Wudgut spat on the floor. Not a flicker later, the spectres reappeared, seemingly empowered in a clear glassy light that shed its lustre into every shadow.

"Thy benevolence, though lacking the humour of frequented civility be as consistent as our memory of it. Is that not correct, Mr S?"

"Indeed so, Mr S. Tis enough to make our new found fewness unavailable for any requirement of misconduct pertinent to his future needs. Tis injurious and inconsiderate that were we fit in any way to suffer it, we would. Is that not so, Mr S?"

"Indeed it is, Mr S. Indeed it is."

Wudgut remained seated. Spiffle sidled to the curtain. I remained where hospitality had instructed.

The Pegs persisted. "We are made here to report a treachery that loyalty betrayed hath seen fit to confiscate that by which we are better met in this world. Thus tis we are resigned from a life fond as any and banished against our will to a nameless place, wherein all that we desire be elsewhere. Is that not so, Mr S?"

"Indeed it is, Mr S. Tis our unhappy duty to report a poison at work in all of this and to lament how tis, in this world, that the lives of some require the lives of others, as if all that is made a mystery by it hath failed in their vacuous hearts."

Wudgut interrupted their breathless chant by raising a hand. He spoke. His tone unchanged. "How is it the great weight of so much language can equal nothing? Plainly, gentlemen, thy fates hath tainted thy rhetoric. For not a word of the thousands defecated into thy gibberish containeth any substance."

"If thy boundless benevolence will allow thee to reconsider, reason will reveal such a judgement to be baseless. Twould appear to me that the meaning of our message be somewhat shrouded by good manners, but little else, and never was their intent anything other than a disclosure of what it is they carry. Have we not served thee by the same good measure these years passed?"

"Indeed we have, Mr S. With little reward for the sacrifice of it, conspiring the while to betray such duty with obscure deceptions that hath left us imprisoned by nothing more than our will to assist others. It is a great misfortune and one for which we are undeserving."

Wudgut stood up. "What be undeserved, gentlemen, is your snivelling presence in this place. As for misfortune, twas always mine to suffer it regarding any undertaking requiring your unshrinkable inattention to all things relevant. Never was an employer more misled by incompetence. As for thy garbled wordwork, never was it more failed than now."

The Pegs were unmoved. "Never were we the beneficiaries of any good will on your part. Yet did we persist in our commitment to the tasks required, no matter how troublesome. Our abilities to abandon the physical constraints of our bodies whilst asleep were a prize never intended for the use to which thy acquaintance subverted it. Twas a harmless art. Tranquil. Gifted to appease the day to day of things. Not pry and poke into the business of others not deserving such underhand attention by merit of its concealment from them. Is that not correct, Mr S?"

"Indeed so, Mr S. Indeed so. And if the heartless are witless to boot, let them now claim such clarity as gibberish. For no better could the shameful mix of it be revealed. We have been most cruelly poisoned, sir. Poisoned. By a winged thingywhatsit."

"A small thinged wingywhatsit."

Wudgut moved to one side. He pointed directly at me. "A winged thingywhatsit such as this?"

The Pegs turned, appearing at first not to notice my presence, in what was now a fierce light. They hovered close. After a scrutinising stare, they reassumed their former position before Wudgut. "Similar."

"Remarkably similar, Mr S."

"Indeed so, Mr S."

"An identical hindrance of legs. Same height, hair, eyes, wings. Remarkable indeed."

Wudgut stepped slowly toward his oven. Spiffle was

almost entirely concealed by the curtain.

The Pegs continued. "Such a creature did we find, yet was ours hindered with appurtenances befriending our door in such a manner as to confine our responsibilities. No swifter could a stranger avail themselves of an invitation offered than she was party to that by which all things find benefit in this world. Then to our consternation and without provocation, lest politeness and good manners cause offence, did she name that which we prize above all as common water. Filthy, disgusting water. Infested by all manner of things that have rolled off the edge of the world into its corruption. Was that not so Mr S?"

"Indeed it was Mr S. Indeed it was. That was what she claimed it to be." There was a moment's silence. "I have a notion Mr S. A notion that we may have judged the guiltless guilty. What if the winged thingywhatsit was as truthful as she claimed? Strange hath turned to stranger yet. Did we not anticipate such a find in such a place? Hid so well as a moment lost. Warnings claim a dubious truth Mr S. A dubious truth. Tis possible we have been poisoned by water. Hence our souls be washed away."

"A notion shared Mr S. A notion shared. Yet that which binds us to this answer doth also seal our fate. As for guilt, let us be generous with it Mr S. Generous. For here are we guilty all. Let us persist whilst intent and determination doth endure. Water hath placed us beyond persecution. If the guilty are to suffer, suffer they shall." Twas the final provocation. Wudgut swore and stamped upon the floor. Rage spat words twixt the grit of his teeth as he pulled a long iron bar from the shelf of his oven. Screaming at the apparitions bloomed before him he lashed into them with a fearsome stroke that cut the air as would the breath of a curse. There was a blinding flash. An intense flare of cruel light, so vivid, so bright that all within it was lost to the eye. I heard Wudgut stumble. His weapon fall. Then was a great blackness set upon the chamber, so still, so profound, that were all the stories of the world consumed within it not a word or picture would be known.

## 72

For some time I sat in darkness unable to persuade myself to move. Where was Wudgut? Where was Spiffle? Twas such a black event even reason be hid. Cautiously I sniffed for clues. It revealed little. Twas as though in all the dark days of this man's death had he collected every passing shadow into the vacancy once occupied by his life. Were I seized into the blackest stone, no surer could my quest be stalled. Then was there stirred into the mix of this isolation a voice. Remote. Almost out of hearing. Yet known as if it sat below night's horizon like the promise of a new day. With sombre whispers did it shake the dark as would a chiming bell its ancient shadow. Twas the voice of my father.

"Much travelled am I of late. From morn to middlemust and dust. Yet never was a night better spent than this. How a moon doth our darkness eat, thus containing that which desired to contain us all. Look and nothing will ye see, for tis by darkness am I better met. By Morichel am I known. Or Melchior, or not. Water on stone, black dog dead, noseless face, hat on head. Red clay clinched, suffocate a soul, dogstar lit, lead bloodbowl. Where does a day but by desires untold abandon thee?"

"Father?"

"Best count thy steps if ye wish to acquire the measure of this place. Darkness doth collude a gathering to vanquish any spirit in this land. A fury unknowing even of its own desire. Not contained by circle or square."

"Father?"

"Great was the burden of my life. The unbearable disappointment of its false trail. A labyrinth of my own making. Were I to count the nothingness of it, twould be best reckoned. Able to pass its likeness through the world of living things. Hardly a cloud's shadow, yet known to all. Set the obscurity of its face toward a fated world. Listen. Eternity be ever so hushed. Indifferent to the clamour of all else. I have seen thee well enough. Reflected even in thine eyes, yet unseen by haste as things lost in water. Formless are we formed to all. Thus tis a soul be cast to grimy chance. Rebuked by the cutting of flesh whose scars have well counted the toll of my folly hid within another's head. Not by a yellow cup or the bark of a card could this be seen to flicker in another quarter."

"Father?"

"Fear not. Mr Wudgut be cut to size. Or sized to the cut. Thy talisman hath repealed thy fortune by this night's work. Look into that which by love hath sheltered thy soul in this quest. If truth be but a glimmer, then darkness will reveal it. Boiled or buried or pricked with a pin, thin as mole's blood will the egg of thy soul secure it."

Twas then an ember of hope began to deceive the shrouded air. One light, then two, followed by a third. Set to glow upon the floor.

"What water hath taken it will repair. What be absorbed — let loose. Made invisible — seen again. Illuminated thy sins — swallow thee whole."

So tis a wink doth snitch on a sin, and that which by spritish guile once given — seen again. Tourmeline, amber and quartz lay upon the bone like embers spilt from Wudgut's oven. Soon was the skull better lit. Vacant of any immediate threat, I hurriedly recovered my coat, securing it by buckle and button to that which none uncursed would part it. Hastily I gripped the bar to bob the lead that plugged the head. By a singular effort was the ball dispatched as the sweat of woodworld sank cold into the moony flush of Wudgut's barrow. Snatching my bow thus springing a blade, I cautiously set apart the curtains where Spiffle had made his exit. Yet was there nothing but dirt and bone. Returning to the gems, was I swift to hang them as a lamp to the ladder. Never was my soul made more free than by my scurried departure from that place. And as I escaped into the night, any threat without was well hid by the spectre cast from that merciless skull across mine own.

## 73

Twas the ghost of a morning that struggled to evict the last of night. Pale as pity in a goblin's heart. Sheltered neath a stone was it less easy to imagine my safety than the offer afforded. The voice of my father, words that were spoken, the disembodied Pegs, Wudgut and Spiffle's disappearance. All of these and more it seemed tempered for the first time by a hunger within, as though my body were emptied of all things. Tis doubtful my humour would improve, though served with silver on a table of flint. This land hath made everything unsure. Voices carry back and forth for want of a head. But wait. What is this? In my eagerness to evade entrapment I had almost forgotten... the jewels. Repaired into my possession yet again by some unknown agency. Removing them from my pocket, I held them up against a frail light to determine their authenticity. Liberty hath not freed me of my suspicions, as anything in this land may reflect a better truth elsewhere. Yet secured inside could plain be seen the bit of a bat—a glove, a hat, locked by wordweight and fire within quartz and tourmaline. Tis reassuring that such distances cannot falter endorsements bonded thus. Twas then I noticed the amber too had acquired within its moony make a blot o' blood. A reddish core. Difficult to see. Turning myself about enabled what light there was to better penetrate the glaze allowing me to discover what lay within. How a moon doth our darkness eat. Thus containing that which desired to contain us all. For set before my disbelief was the entirety of Wudgut plain seen, fastened by enchantment into the stony fracture of its heart. How such a consummation found its mark, I know not. There be little cause for me to question such benevolence. Yet was I beset by uncertainty. For never was a realm more likely to make one doubt thine own reflection. Perhaps imagination bribed by hope did hear my father tell me Wudgut's fate. That he be truly cut to size, or sized to the cut.

I sat for most of the afternoon staring at the constriction of his image. The entirety of his shameful misbehaviour stranded seamless in the palm of my hand. The whole substance of his cruel and injurious life squeezed into no less chilled a heart. His figure stooped, a hand risen as though to shield his eyes. A moment locked (I suspected) by a key that no amount of time will tempt to undo. Such flawless evil truly met. The mischief of his make ensnared within an eye no less significant than his mother's. Tis often said that that which ye consume consumeth thee.

And what of the Pegs? To what expense did their lives accommodate within the amber such menace? Lives linked by employment to Wudgut, consumed with regret. Had such an incumbency finally undone their double edged ambition? And the voice. The voice of my father? Vapourish, rueful. Weariness and dejection cloaking his words, as though their very meaning be hid. Yet met as a kiss once offered. My very life reminded where its frailty lay. Such talk as knew his disillusioned heart. A gloom wherein the lives of those closest to him remained unheard. What favours there be to gain from all this tis impossible to say. And Spiffle. Where be Spiffle? His dramas of entrance and exit no better lit, but no better seen. Evaporated into the everyday like a hat in a rock or a glove in an eye. Bound by a life of servitude to that which I suspect by some hidden design was in turn of service to him. Was his choice to refuse benevolence from any quarter an indication of a lack of ambition or ambition itself? Too weary to weigh the half of it, I chewed on a spit o' specklespin. As night approached, the way ahead fraught by such double dealing loomed double dark.

# 74

Night, yet no night in a treeless wood. A great basin of space. A bowl of wingwonder were I fit to face it with due merit. Scoured by owls. Three be my guess. Maybe four. Their tone almost indistinguishable from the flutes of elves. Tis their language that be entirely at odds. The calls of these creatures haunting the air like a summons from the dead. Tis not the joy of a jig that most will hear before their death upon this leafy stage. I will need to exercise caution, lest the breath of the hunter fills my nostrils. Yet owls be honest enough. Even so, tis a gracious space after so long a confinement, exposing the glister of endlessness in a roof wrought of hallfame. Keeping to the centre, I followed a fair path through new grass and old wood until I happened on a tiny brook. The entire perimeter ably retained by the continued calls, better allowing me to define as direct a path as possible.

For three nights did I travel without hindrance. The weather fair kept, the days secured at rest. But by the fourth night a great entanglement of thornlunge fouled my momentum and I was reduced to a crawl along woven ways. A cruel corridor for so full a house. I was well into the darkened stitch of it when I confronted a creature dark of cloth and dark of skin. The iridescence of its turquoise hair, glimpsed as would the passing moment of a distant summer in the memory. Its eyes unseen, yet seeing nonetheless. The silhouette of its walk constant as one's shadow. Its sour voice, sinking every word into the disappearance of its make.

"Who be thou, if I be Skwookan Owlgloo? For thou art as partial as all things to me."

I offered up my name.

"I have never heard it, though slept on stone or dreamt of a ladder. I have a room within this place, black as a poisoned tongue, though by fairer fortune blessed with stool and chair. I have a sword of faction, yet am disarmed by uncertainties. Indistinct as ye be, I offer by the boil of a feather a host's comfort."

Side by side, we made our way down a dry louring aisle. Thorn, dust and shadow hatched. Path woven did we finally descend upon the apprehension of another skull. Though this one be lost for doors. The only lock — that of its resting place. Dog by make. Its four surviving teeth walling in the roof of its mouth, along which we approached the open door of its rear. Within the pan twas smooth and clean. A stool of polished stone, a chair fashioned from the severed hand of a mole. Cupped into a natural seat, the five blades of its fingers, too close by my reckoning for any comfort afforded. A store of berries. A table of thorny tools. Little else.

"Sit. As I be partially hid to thee, then thou art hid to me. The stuff of thy everyday veiled somewhat out of fashion. Watch."

Plucking the eyes from its head did it blindly juggle the red beads with deft skill before popping them back into their sockets.

"Thou art no better seen by such a trick than when first we met. Half seen, half heard, the yardstick by which I judge the entirety. Am I real as real can be? Or only what a wish will see? Nothing more, nothing less. Only what a wish confess."

Claiming its seat was I offered sustenance. Perched upon the white pebble, did I imbibe all that from the berry was offered. Far from black, the skull was surprisingly light, considering its disorder, netted deep in a havoc of thorns.

"This estate be woven to taste. Half my life spent in such a place, whilst the other half looked for it—or looked to leave it. I know not which. For tis a thought careless as breeze. Tis possible we have met, having never done so. Surely such a notion balance thy reasoning too."

I confessed to the possibility of such encounters. For was this land not overly unsettled by such vapid uncertainties.

"Tis a realm defended by terrible things. A course kept is a course plundered. Yet stray from it, and by no darker menace will thy light be snuffed. Resolution be thy best bet, even half seen. For half blinded, am I half as likely to misread such warnings as defend or inability to read 'em. The elves are close."

Immediately my hopes were raised, and I enquired as to a direction.

"One direction be as another. Perhaps sleep will clear thy path as good as any told. Repose a while, yet rest assured at dark's approach I will awaken thee."

Overburdened by troublesome thoughts I lay against the curve of the wall, wrapped within my inheritance, fatigued and foot weary. In no time was my host and I danced identical, stepping from one foot to another, changing worlds.

## 75

I awoke to night's repeated threat. Owlgloo sat upon the matted hand, present yet vanished. Its startle of hair fired silver atop a silhouette of repose.

"Were I to spit or bleed upon stone, thy mind would be no less twiddly. Ease the knots of thy talisman, so shall ye ease thy passage. Tis as sure as a tangle tumble thee to trouble, or a break still thy heart. The greatest of doors be set to seal the fate of many, yet thou art small enough to escape by its keyhole. Take care—lest ye unwittingly destroy that for which relentlessly ye have searched. If the red of the head be blood not hair, perhaps evil hath struck thee yet. Fingers will fall for so foul a deed. I have seen the cuckoo's footman. The wolfchild, white hatted— drink its own urine. Tie a knot to raise a cloud, by widdershins the fairest shadows found. Thou hast travelled far—yet never from thy true desire. Who is hid from who in so poor a pot as this? For that which looks without a single fear sees furthest."

Owlgloo then gestured for the gemmed twine to be suspended from a hook of iron wormed through the skull's roof. Spun with some force were the stones then hurled into a fierce orbit.

"Thus are we set upon the wheel that binds eternity with indifference. Whose words are these—forked so sharp as to catch wisdom unawares? Something much seen by me but less by thee. A talisman such as this containeth many shadows. Fire hath the blackest heart. Yet are we much acquainted. Each disposed to the other by a fondle of fate. When much occurs, little is seen. Yet the shadow doth mimic it eternal. So it is every action binds thee hence."

And with this cant Owlgloo abruptly vanished. Even the lustre of its hair unseen, gathered in moments by imagination but little else. Immediately the stones lit anew, scattering a race of colours over the bony bowl as they continued at speed to revolve above my head. But as their splendour intensified, their pace lessened, promptly stilling their fiery path to a stationary luminosity that left not a shadow undriven. Owlgloo reappeared into this vividness black as all the letters having spelt the haunted moments of this realm. Snatching the gems, he carefully mounted the stone of his seat. Removing the slippery fixtures of his eyes yet again, he replaced the precarious balls of red jelly with the radiant tourmaline and quartz. Then to my consternation did he swallow the amber containing the wizened Wudgut in a single gulp. Gesturing with his hand for me to remain quietly seated, did he repair to the severed clutch of Mr Mole. As his new eyes reduced their glory, the chamber gradually darkened. Shadows crept imperceptible as fate for the familiar expectations of not knowing.

"This be a night well poised to swallow the weak of the world. The great maze of its crooked hand, cooked as a web o'er the willow-wand of this moon's dance, dull as a corpse candle. So shall the deeds of such a night pass undetected through its ghostly eye. The cruel-natured cleanse their hands of sin in the silver bowl of its countenance. I who was burdened to carry my own heart rotting in a common sack, preserved by fire of salt, did answer the riddle that spelt the complexity of my loss—a lifetime's measure. The elves are but a day's distance from where we sit. Thou hast endured thy will—yet endured by it."

So twas we parted. And not a day passed 'fore I dined with silver on a table of grey flint. The elves keen to hear my story—yet keener still to end it as had been desired. Yet how can such a story as this ever end—except by life's last breath?

# About the Author

M J Westley's lifelong artistic endeavour has been primarily with the visual arts: drawing and painting. After leaving college, he travelled through Morocco before returning to work in repertory theatre until 1975, when he undertook a postgrad course at Cardiff College of Art. Through the 80's and 90's, he worked in a variety of jobs that included theatre, advertising, driving, gardening and teaching. He also rode his motorcycle across most of Western Europe and Ireland. Exhibitions of his drawings were held in cities throughout the UK. In 1992, he won the Guinness Prize at the Royal Academy, leading to increased exhibitions of his work in London.

Since 1996 (the year his son was born) the corpus of his work has been landscape paintings. Based in the West Midlands, he travels throughout the country on his motorbike, covering thousands of miles, collecting material for future works. He has also written poems and stories, as well as a strange biographical work entitled *Prospographical Strains*. *Thimblestar* took seven years to write, between all the paintings, drawings and travel.

On the creation of *Thimblestar*, he says: "The whole thing hinges on its relationship with my grandfather. In the novel, it is he who is given the story and he alone able to decipher its enigmatic 'codes'. Although Grandfather writes the story, it was related to him by an elemental. English is not the language of faeries, but over thousands of years these creatures have assimilated it well enough. As the story progresses, it is well to bear in mind this provenance, which although it doesn't explain any of the strange language does provide a reason why it is the way it is."

M J Westley's art web site: www.mjwestley.co.uk

# IMMANION PRESS

## Purveyors of Speculative Fiction

### Night's Nieces: The Legacy of Tanith Lee

 In the footsteps of the High Priestess of Fantasy... Tanith Lee was a huge influence on fantasy literature, and a generation of writers were captivated by her iconic prose and surreal visions. Here is a collection of stories by female writers, for whom Tanith Lee was a friend and mentor, as well as an inspiration. Each 'niece' has written a short story inspired by Tanith's work, as well as an accompanying article. The book also includes previously unpublished photographs from Tanith's life, as well as artwork by the authors.

*Contributors include Storm Constantine, Cecilia Dart-Thornton, Vera Nazarian, Sarah Singleton, Kari Sperring, Sam Stone, Freda Warrington and Liz Williams. With an introduction by Tanith's husband, John Kaiine.*
ISBN: 978-1-907737-71-8 £11.99, $18.99

### The Moonshawl by Storm Constantine

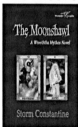 Ysbryd drwg... the bad ghost. Hired by Wyva, the phylarch of the Wyvachi tribe, Ysobi goes to Gwyllion to create a spiritual system based upon local folklore, but soon discovers some of that folklore is out of bounds, taboo... Secrets lurk in the soil of Gwyllion, and the old house Meadow Mynd. The fields are soaked in blood and echo with the cries of those who were slaughtered there, almost a century ago. Old hatreds and a thirst for vengeance have been awoken by the approaching coming of age of Wvya's son, Myvyen. If the harling is to survive, Ysobi must lay the ghosts to rest and scour the tainted soil of malice. But the ysbryd drwg is strong, built of a century of resentment and evil thoughts. Is it too powerful, even for a scholarly hienama with Ysobi's experience and skill? *The Moonshawl* is a standalone supernatural story, set in the world of Storm Constantine's ground-breaking, science fantasy Wraeththu mythos. ISBN: 978-1-907737-62-6 £11.99, $20.99

## Immanion Press
http://www.immanion-press.com
info@immanion-press.com

# Through the Night Gardens

## A Transmedia Project by Storm Constantine

**https://throughthenightgardens.wordpress.com/**

'Through the Night Gardens' is a new transmedia project by fantasy writer, Storm Constantine.

The chapters of the story will appear as 'episodes' on a new blog, (address above), which are free to read. Each will have an accompanying landscape – created using the 'dimension' building feature from the online role-playing game, Rift – which can be visited and explored in the free-to-play game, should readers wish to do so. Screenshots from the landscapes will also appear within the story chapters.

This project brings a new dimension to storytelling. An audio book and accompanying videos are also being planned, with the chapters of the story eventually being published – with new characters and sub plots – as a full length novel in printed form and eBook.

The first chapter, 'The House on the Red Cliffs', was published in December 2015, with an additional five chapters to follow. Full information, and the story itself, can be found on the blog.

In association with Immanion Press
http://www.immanion-press.com

# NEWCON PRESS

http://newconpress.co.uk/

## The very best in fantasy, science fiction, and horror

### Azanian Bridges by Nick Wood

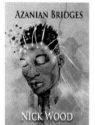

In a modern day South Africa where Apartheid still holds sway, Sibusiso Mchunu, a young amaZulu man, finds himself the unwitting focus of momentous events when he falls foul of the system and comes into possession of a secret that may just offer hope to his entire people. Pursued by the ANC on one side and Special Branch agents on the other, Sibusiso has little choice but to run.

Azanian Bridges is a truly ground-breaking book from South African-born author Nick Wood. This, his debut novel, is a socially acute fast-paced thriller that propels the reader into a world of intrigue and threat, leading to possibilities that examine the conscience of a nation.

ISBN: 978-1-910935-11-8 (limited ed. Signed hardback) £24.99
ISBN: 978-1-910935-12-5 (paperback) £11.99

*"A very good novel indeed; the emotional intelligence is as high as its political insightfulness – the whole is compelling and moving." – Adam Roberts*

### Splinters of Truth by Storm Constantine

Storm Constantine is one of our finest writers of genre fiction. This new collection, *Splinters of Truth*, features fifteen stories, four of them original to this volume, that transport the reader to richly imagined realms one moment and shine a light on our own world's darkest corners the next. A writer of rare passion, Storm delivers here some of her most accomplished work to date.

*"Storm Constantine is a myth-making Gothic queen, whose lush tales are compulsive reading. Her stories are poetic, involving, delightful and depraved. I wouldn't swap her for a dozen Anne Rices." – Neil Gaiman*

ISBN: 978-1-910935-07-1 (limited ed signed hardback) £24.99
ISBN: 978-1-907069-84-0 (paperback) £12.99

Lightning Source UK Ltd.
Milton Keynes UK
UKOW04f1343200316

270515UK00003B/38/P